MY JOB?

Praise for the book

"Learnability is the most important tool to stay relevant in today's changing work environment. Sunil Mishra's book captures the self-discovery of a person to find exciting opportunities amidst roller-coaster transformation... the future of work could be different, and probably more interesting."

—*Prof. Debashis Chatterjee*
Director, IIM Kozhikode; Mentor Director, IIM Amritsar

"The book captures the change in employment pattern from big IT companies to startups. With the rise of AI and machine learning, the future of work is increasingly tilting in favor of startups. The very high growth of startups, heavy spending on technology and marketing will accelerate employment in this sector."

—*T.V. Mohandas Pai*
Chairman, Aarin Capital and Manipal Global Education

"Offers a fascinating ground level view of the transformations that Indian IT has gone through and what lies ahead. It isn't going to be easy for anyone and there is no clear outcome. But it is important to understand the issues, technological and cultural."

—*Vivek Wadhwa*
Distinguished Fellow at Harvard Law School

WHO STOLE MY JOB?

SUNIL MISHRA

Srishti
PUBLISHERS & DISTRIBUTORS

SRISHTI PUBLISHERS & DISTRIBUTORS
Registered Office: N-16, C.R. Park
New Delhi – 110 019
Corporate Office: 212A, Peacock Lane
Shahpur Jat, New Delhi – 110 049
editorial@srishtipublishers.com

First published by
Srishti Publishers & Distributors in 2019

10 9 8 7 6 5 4 3 2 1

Printed and bound in India

Dedicated to
my mother and father.

Acknowledgement

Digital disruption is a hot topic of discussion in many IT companies today. I am thankful to my colleagues and friends who have directly or indirectly contributed to the conversation on the topic that has inspired this story. I have constantly bothered many of them while sharing ideas and stories from the book. It has been great to get encouragement from them.

I acknowledge the inputs on overall plot and characters provided by my friend Neeraj Sinha. He has been kind enough to read through the early drafts more than once and provide significant comments. I am also thankful to Rajesh Shankaran, an author himself, and Milind Kolhatkar, an avid reader who went through my manuscript and provided relevant inputs. My ten-year-old son also read through the book and provided useful inputs at times.

I am grateful to Mr. Vivek Wadhwa, Mr. T.V. Mohandas Pai and Professor Debashis Chatterjee for taking out time from their extremely busy schedules to scan through the book and provide some encouraging words.

Publishing a book is never an easy task. Thanks to Arup Bose from Srishti Publishers who accepted my book proposal and provided valuable inputs during the publishing process. Finally, I am grateful to Stuti, my editor, who has diligently gone through each and every word of the book several times, to make sure the overall story comes out well.

The CEO

"You are still panting. Have a sip of water and relax," Satvik told Ajesh, offering him his water bottle.

"I hate 'missing the bus', both literally and figuratively," replied Ajesh.

"Monday morning is tough for everyone," said Satvik, "this time we had a long weekend as well. To catch this 7:30 a.m. bus, I have to wake up at 6 a.m. and run through the daily routines in an hour."

"But you are always well on time, Satvik. I have never seen you running late like me," said Ajesh taking the aisle seat near Satvik as the bus driver closed the automatic door with a creak.

"Look at the positive side of it, Ajesh. The company bus motivates you to get some morning exercise and adds a bit of excitement."

"Very true. Jokes apart, I must say that the company bus service is one of the best gifts an employee can get in Bengaluru. Creative Tech is possibly the best company when it comes to employee welfare," Ajesh said.

"Yes, I agree," said Satvik. "However when I compare it with my father's company, it still fails the test."

"And which is that company?"

"Tata, they not only took care of their employees, but almost set up the entire city – from roads to hospitals, dams to schools. I grew up in the steel city of Jamshedpur that was a corporate social project by itself. They even went beyond employees for the welfare of nearby villagers. My father had colleagues who were 3rd generation employees. My father had insisted that I join the same company and we work as a proud father-son duo," replied Satvik.

"Your benchmark is altogether different, but don't forget those were manufacturing companies of the past. We are in the digital age now. This is not the era of lifelong employment. In the last sixteen years, I have changed five companies. It's not something I wanted, but this is how things work these days," replied Ajesh.

"That's okay," added Satvik, "but the key values don't change over time. While the companies expect the best output from their employees, the employees want a predictable and stable life. That's how organizations live beyond generations, even though business cycles keep fluctuating."

"Predictability and stability is a mirage these days in IT companies."

Concluding this short conversation, Ajesh pulled out the newspaper from his bag. It was the best time to catch up with the daily news.

For Satvik, the one hour bus ride to office was thinking time, probably the best time to reflect about everything in life – be it career, work, family or anything else. The only thing he prayed for was not to be seated next to someone who was on a conference call with his or her team – a terrible morning in that case.

The start of the day in the office used to be very quiet, especially on Monday morning. As Satvik was the first one to arrive on his floor, he switched on the lights of his cubicle.

He reluctantly logged into his laptop to check emails. There were 242 unread mails in the inbox. Hmm... side effects of the long weekend.

"I have told my team not to mark me in the mail unless there is an action expected from me in particular, but many still mark me with one cryptic word 'FYI only," Satvik thought. He had to do something about it.

"I will propose a penalty of ten rupees for every unwanted mail from any of my team members."

The first mail was an automated one – reminding him of all the pending actions last week – delete. Over a period of time, Satvik had built a habit of deleting all the system triggered mails, even though it got him into trouble sometimes. There was another mail to participate in employee satisfaction survey – delete. These are all irritants, he thought.

The third mail was slightly unusual. Satvik clicked it open. It was addressed to all the staff of the company.

From: Chairman's office
To: All Staff of Creative Tech

Sub: Welcoming our new CEO

Dear Friends,

It gives me immense pleasure to welcome our new CEO, Marshal Scott. He is an industry veteran with over thirty years of experience in various leadership roles in different IT organizations. In his previous roles, he has been a technocrat, a product head, chief digital officer and business unit head with top line and bottom line responsibilities. Marshal brings a global perspective with extensive experience in the US and Europe, where he has successfully managed the business earlier.

*I am sure Marshal will help Creative Tech speed up the digital
transformation that is currently underway.*

*Marshal holds multiple patents in banking technologies.
He is a computer science graduate from Carnegie Mellon
University. His hobbies include scuba diving, baseball and
American football. He will be based in the Palo Alto office.*

*I also take this opportunity to thank Arvind Shankar,
for the immense contribution that he has made to Creative
Technologies during the last two years as CEO. We all wish
him very best for future endeavours.*

"Did you look at Marshal's LinkedIn profile?" Ajesh asked. "It is really
inspirational. Someone with a Carnegie Mellon background has been
selected as Creative Tech CEO – there couldn't have been a better
appointment in these turbulent times."

Satvik realized there were a few things in the mail quite expected,
and few things new. The big talk of digital transformation was the
usual mumbo-jumbo. Every leader had been talking about it since the
last few years, though most had faltered in real results. The choice of
an American CEO based in US was slightly unusual, at least it was a
first for a Bengaluru based IT company that was a shining beacon in
the India story.

"Could they not find anyone from the fifty thousand employees
to head this iconic company?" Satvik asked Ajesh.

Satvik had spent fifteen years with Creative Tech. He had seen
its heydays when the company was growing at breathtaking speed. It
looked unstoppable from all aspects. As a blue chip company, it also
took great care of its employees. It became more like a social set-up
for him over time and a great place to work as well.

Ajesh, on the other hand, was a recent hire in the company. He
had professional experience with many similar companies, more
importantly, those undergoing digital transformations.

"How much time on an average do you spend daily on LinkedIn? We should all rename you as LinkedIn Ajesh," Satvik teased Ajesh.

"These days you are professionally as good as you look on LinkedIn. I have already sent my invite to Marshal."

With regards to the choice of the American CEO, Ajesh said, "Our previous CEO was an Indian. Did that really make any difference?"

He added, "What matters most is the knowledge about the industry, market and ability to lead during difficult times. Moreover, if we have the aspiration to become a global organization, we need not be too particular about these things. Even the choice of the CEO's office in the US is in tune with current realities. The leaders should be based where the bulk of our business action is and drive innovations through our clients."

Very often, Satvik and Ajesh would differ on the interpretations of key decisions and events in the organization. The funny thing was that none of them had any influence on those decisions. It just provided juice for some intellectual conversations during the lunch time and tea-breaks.

Satvik and Ajesh both were middle level managers with a stagnant title of 'Senior Project Manager'. They were, in essence, like a half-broken bridge that still connected thousands of software engineers with the top management. They were too junior to decide on the company policies, at the same time, too senior to criticize them openly. They not only had an unbreakable glass ceiling, but also a slippery glass floor.

Satvik remembered how quickly he had got promotions during his early days in Creative Tech. He was also awarded 'Employee of the Year' once for completing his assigned task well before the project deadline. This helped the New Indian Bank in avoiding a hefty fine from Reserve Bank of India. Satvik still had all those awards and plaques proudly displayed in his cubicle. Reminiscing the glorious days, Satvik looked at the framed photographs and rearranged them one more time.

For all the difficult times the organization was facing currently, Satvik still felt a fond association with Creative Tech. For him, Creative Tech was more than a mere workplace; it was a place where he started his professional career fifteen years ago. Most of his close friends were his colleagues. He loved his work. Once a friend asked him if Creative Tech had a good work-life balance.

"When you enjoy work, it becomes your life," Satvik had responded promptly.

"Do you have any more information about this new CEO decision?" Satvik asked Vikas, his manager.

"No, but there were some coffee-corner discussions that the Creative Tech CEO role has been jinxed for the last five years. After all, this is the third such change," replied Vikas with a giggle.

"You know, the biggest problem now is to explain this change to our team, who would believe that we have complete information about it."

"Well that is what managers are paid for," Vikas replied, "for managing the team without clear information."

Instead of the usual task allocation and status check, Satvik's weekly team meeting was full of questions.

"Is there any risk to the employees in India, given that there are rumors of scaling up US operations?" Radhika asked.

Satvik had also heard such rumours. In fact, Ajesh had told him that in his previous organization, the CEO had started a similar focused drive to hire employees in the US, mainly to accelerate innovations and market adoption.

The increased US hiring policy for Indian IT companies always baffled Satvik. He had grown in the organization, making a business case for US banks – how an offshore development would help them save cost as well as spur innovation. What had changed in recent times – have we changed the nature of our work? Had the American salaries gone down? Our Indian salaries have hardly increased. For a moment, Satvik felt like blurting out to the team –

"My cost analysis says, for every one person hired in the US, we can hire four people in India at the similar expertise level. If they do what you guys are saying, it will be suicidal for Creative Tech."

With great difficulty, Satvik controlled his thoughts one more time and parroted a roundabout response, "We are undergoing a huge digital disruption and leadership is managing this transformation by some very innovative approaches."

Words like 'digital', 'disruption', 'innovation' and 'transformation' were handy jargon to confuse a restive team whenever they got aggressive and inquisitive at such occasions.

Satvik's final addendum was, "This is the best that our management could think of at this hour. Are you with the company or against it?"

There could be only one practical response to a question like this.

"Satvik, I want to ask one question." Akhil raised his hand when the meeting was about to end.

"We often hear phrases like 'management has decided', 'management has agreed', etc. They are used by everyone in our company, from our CEO to our immediate manager like you. But we have never seen this proverbial management whom we can ask genuine questions. Is this term 'management' a ghost?" Akhil teased Satvik's attempt to circumvent any discussion on this topic.

"A very funny question. Can we get back to our daily tasks now? You still have four tickets pending from last week, they are overdue already," Satvik patted Akhil on his shoulder mildly.

Satvik had heard from his father about the fiery management-worker conflicts in the plant. The workplace was a battleground for both. Luckily, in this white collar IT job, there were no such divisions.

They all worked like one big family. Satvik felt happy for once that there were some good things in these IT companies as well.

It was a long eventful day for Satvik. When he reached home late at night, his wife Neeraja told him, "The landlady had come, and said she is going to increase the rent this time by 20 percent."

"We will shift to another house! This is ridiculous!" replied Satvik.

"Shifting is easy for you, not for me and our kids. What happened to your promotion?" Neeraja asked.

"Neeraja, we will soon buy our own house, something that we have been planning since years."

"Honey, planning with you has only one serious drawback – it continues to be a plan always," Neeraja went into the kitchen to prepare dinner.

Employee Town Hall

"I have never seen this auditorium so crowed. Good that we came early," Satvik told Ajesh who was sitting by his side.

"I am surprised to see so many people here, since the entire town hall is being webcast live and everyone can watch from his own seat online," replied Ajesh.

"I think most employees want to see our new CEO physically."

The first town hall with Marshall was nothing short of a gala affair in the company. All the global offices were connected on streaming video-conference. The huge auditorium was packed to capacity. Additional giant screens were put up at many places within the office premises, including food courts and common areas.

Creative Tech had one of the best and enviable infrastructures among Indian companies. The multi-level auditorium was nothing short of the modern, state-of-the-art gigantic movie theatres that could house more than three thousand people at one time. It was nothing short of a festive atmosphere.

Marshal's first interaction with employees was quite unique. He walked up to the stage in black jeans and a light blue T-shirt – a very casual appearance. While many employees were decked in formals and business suits, Marshal appeared an odd man out.

Marshal, a man in his early fifties hopped up the stairs and adjusted the microphone to his height. The image on the giant screen magnified it several times. Even before he spoke a word, there was a loud cheer from the employees, then there was pin drop silence. The last time employees had seen a similar cheering crowd was when Rahul Dravid, the legendary Indian batsman had visited the campus.

The employees were used to someone reading the long list of achievements to introduce an eminent person on stage. Marshal's introduction was different. They played a small video on the giant screen where a middle-aged person was playing with his water-mask in deep sea while scuba diving.

The next video showed Marshal playing golf and later squash. It ended with a beautiful family photograph of Marshal, his wife and two daughters with the background of Statue of Liberty. This was quite unique and an interesting way to introduce the new CEO.

"This is the difference between an Indian and American CEO – they think of more things than just work," Ajesh was quick to comment.

"Very refreshing to see this and I am sure he will have equally good leadership skills, just like his diverse interests," Satvik replied.

Satvik saw the merit in Ajesh's arguments.

"We Indians take work too seriously. There is hardly any focus on work-life balance. I remember when this question was put up to Arvind, our last CEO – 'What do you feel about work life balance in our company?' His prompt reply was, 'We all need to work hard to have a good life'. Everyone had laughed at the reply, but had also got the message."

This first town hall that Marshall conducted after his appointment was very well received. He spoke about the new innovations in the industry and how it was affecting the work and lives of everyone.

Marshal drew parallels from his experience in manufacturing industry where he briefly worked in the 80s in the US. The large scale mechanization in the factories had changed the nature of work. While some mundane work disappeared, it created several new jobs with higher value addition.

"The IT industry today is going through a similar transition as in the manufacturing industry earlier," Marshal said.

"It is an opportunity for all of us to re-discover Creative Tech and be a pioneer in the new world. I want to inculcate a culture of innovation in our company. Today, I am launching a new scheme 'Ideathon' – best 500 ideas from all of you will be rewarded with a cash prize of 1000 dollars each. I am expecting 50,000 ideas, one from each of you," he added further.

The address was a marked departure from similar meetings with the earlier CEOs, who were mainly concerned about cost reduction and controlling waste. Fresh investments were last in their agenda. Marshal was very articulate; he drew inspirational examples from all walks – starting from his research days at Carnegie Mellon to the most recent book that he had read on human consciousness.

After the initial address, it was the usual time for Q&A. During earlier town halls, this section was mostly omitted due to lack of time. Employees were sure this was deliberate, so as to avoid uncomfortable questions that some of the disgruntled employees might ask. With the organization struggling to grow rapidly for the last few years, many employees blamed the leadership for their woes. For them, the town hall was one real avenue to put the uncomfortable spotlight on these policies and vent out their displeasures.

The HR team, on the other hand, was extra careful that these disgruntled employees did not create undesirable noise on such a public platform. To achieve this, sometimes they accepted only pre-screened questions.

"These pre-screened questions in town hall are all planted by HR, did you know that?" Ajesh said.

"Possibly yes. I have never asked a question in these open forums. I hope none of my team member a stands up. It reflects poorly on managers like us, you know," responded Satvik.

Ajesh stood up. "Welcome, Marshal, to Creative Tech. The question that I have is about the digital disruption that you talked about. We know very well how SMAC (social, mobility, analytics and cloud) have been changing our personal and work life. Do you think if we expand our business in this area, we can be successful in company transformation?"

Marshal had difficulty understanding his accent. Ajesh was one of those who spoke Indian English in American accent, thanks to his stay in the US. It could put off people sometimes, however Marshal patiently responded,

"If you really ask me, the biggest disruption that is happening today is not SMAC that you mentioned. SMAC and Artificial Intelligence are just tools through which these changes are happening. The real transformation that is happening is, in the understanding of ownership in our work and personal life. The biggest advancement in human history happened with the development of property rights. This created what we call 'assets' that people owned and traded. Even the IT industry flourished only after a robust intellectual property framework.

"But today, look around yourself – the largest cab company does not own any cab, the largest hotel booking companies do not own hotels and the largest content creator like Facebook does not own any content. There are scores of examples. The products and services of the yesteryears were created with the ownership concept. The software that we wrote earlier was for some enterprise or consumer to buy and deploy. They would pay for the licence or services for deploying and later owning them.

"The cars that were built earlier were for someone to own and maintain. But actually, if you see, ownership has no value other than providing services. All you care for is safe and enjoyable transportation, not the car per se. We have all heard about the driverless car concept being tested and how this would change the way of life. I would go a step further – a driverless car that owns itself. The car takes a loan from a bank on most attractive terms, sets up EMI based on the future rental incomes, sets aside some money for its maintenance, fuel charges, etc. The car can hire some humans to pay for the software and hardware upgrades and also make a modest profit. If you think carefully, all this can be coded in the software that we make. This is the opportunity that I was talking about when I said disruption.

"In essence, we don't need to own anything, just pay for the services that we use, be it a car or software. This is a paradigm shift."

This was a profound answer to a very pertinent question that got everyone thinking. What Marshal said could very well be true – a car that owns itself, a software that upgrades and maintains itself. However, for Satvik, this explanation raised several other questions.

"If we could write a software just once and it would upgrade and maintain itself, what would happen to majority of the IT workforce? If we ever created a self-managing car, what would happen to Uber, the company that had created disruption in the cab business."

There were several questions that Satvik was struggling with, but town hall was not the place to ask counter questions. Marshal was a visionary leader, and he could explain the disruption and most importantly, motivate everyone to do the right things.

"How do you plan to divide your time between India and US, given that most of your employees are based in India while you will be based in the US?"

Everyone turned around to see a teenage girl asking this question.

Employees were surprised, not at the question, but at the teenager who was asking that, "Since when had Creative Tech started hiring teenagers for coding?"

"She is Rita, Marshal's young daughter – we welcome her into the Creative Tech family," the announcement said, and was followed by loud applause.

Marshal smiled, drank some water from the glass and continued with his reply in a very professional manner, "Most of our clients are still in the US and I prefer to be closer to the clients. Though I will be based in the US, my frequent travel plans would make my base location irrelevant."

"Was it a planted question this time?" It did not matter, Satvik thought, as both the questions and the answers were relevant.

"Our promotions and salaries have been frozen for the last two years, even the bonus payments have been disappointing. While Creative Tech has been paying handsome dividends to shareholders, employees hardly get their dues," one of the employees said.

"Employees are the most important stakeholders in any company. Our policy will be employee first – if they are taken care of, they will keep the clients happy, which will eventually result in better revenues and rewards to shareholders. Creative Tech will keep the employee at the centre of each policy from now on. I have set up a SWAT team that will look into all employee related HR issues and present a report in the next thirty days"

"What is a SWAT team?" Satvik asked Ajesh.

"Oh, you don't know? In the US, this term refers to a group of elite policemen who specialize in high risk tasks like hostage rescue. In common parlance, it is referred to a group of specialists to solve a specific problem."

"Then Marshal is absolutely right, we do need a SWAT team to rescue the poor employees from the clutches of our HR. They are no better than hostage takers," Satvik jokingly whispered in Ajesh's ear.

"I am happy to share that we have earmarked 10% of our wage cost this time for the annual promotion and additional bonus payments. I am also launching a scheme where 1% of our top performing employees will be sent to Carnegie Mellon for four weeks' training on new technologies."

This was the loudest cheer that the employees had ever heard in that auditorium. It was followed by clapping and even some whistling.

"Don't be so happy – these announcements are usually for public consumption. For all that you know, it might be only applicable for some junior software engineers," Satvik told Ajesh.

"At this stage, all that matter is the intent."

"Marshal, you look smart in casual jeans and a T-shirt, but look at us, we are all forced to wear this noose called the 'tie'. The cultural revolutions should start from casual dressing, shouldn't it?" another employee asked.

"Okay, then this is a good time to make this announcement – now onwards Creative Tech will not enforce a formal dress code for employees."

"What a relief!" Ajesh told Satvik.

Satvik and Ajesh had debated this topic earlier. Satvik thought formals at work added a bit of seriousness and sincerity among employees. Ajesh called him outdated for such views.

Next day, *The Business Line* reported,

The new CEO of Creative Tech gets a rock star welcome from employees

It is the first time that Creative Tech has hired an American CEO. This is an opportunity for an Indian enterprise going truly global as Marshal is a well-known leader in the Silicon Valley.

As a first step, Marshal has introduced a series of actions that will help generate tremendous goodwill among the employees. He has announced 10% average hike for all their employees. Some of the top performers have received a personal appreciation mail from the CEO's desk. It was a surprise to these people when they received iPads.

In line with modern management principles, Marshal has got rid of the current appraisal system that force fitted their employees into unproductive 'Bell-curve'. The company plans to replace that with a new continuous assessment program throughout the year.

A slew of employee friendly policies have also been unveiled, e.g. work from home, relaxed dressing, access to social media and no mandatory work hours. Sometimes, it is so easy to fix the discontentment in the organization by doing such small things. Many of them did not even have any financial impact. A listening CEO can quickly uplift the morale of the organization. This was clearly evident from the first few weeks of Marshal's on-boarding.

The new CEO is well set to bring about the much needed cultural change for Creative Tech. The 5% increase in the share price is a testimony that even market is cheering this.

Marshal was happy at this flattering report in the media. He tweeted the link of this report with a message

'Let the journey begin.'

For the first time, Satvik created a twitter account and happily retweeted Marshal's message.

"I will no longer be a social media Luddite," Satvik decided. The new CEO had already brought a fundamental change in the employees.

Satvik was happy that the company was finally taking the right steps on the path to recovery. Leadership makes all the difference, he thought.

New Business Goals

Just four weeks after the new CEO's coming onboard, Satvik received a mail from Vikas, his manager.

From: Vikas Raj
To: Satvik Saxena

Sub: Unit review with Marshal

Satvik,

I received a call from Marshal's office that he wants to review our unit performance during his India visit next week. He has asked us to present the following points for forty-five minutes:

1. *Account revenue projection for next year*
2. *Automation and efficiency improvement plan*
3. *Digital adoption plan*

Let us create a draft plan and deliberate within the team. Since this is our first formal review with the new CEO, we should put our best foot forward. Kindly prioritize this over all other activities.

Regards,
Vikas

Satvik checked the timestamp of the mail; it was sent at 11:30 p.m. He and Vikas met many times during the day. His cabin was right across Satvik's cubicle and they avoided sending emails to each other. It was already too late to call him back and discuss this mail even though it made Satvik worry. One more time Satvik told himself – "It is a bad habit to check emails before going to bed."

Satvik had suspected it was coming sometime – a unit review with the new CEO. However, this was not something that he was really looking forward to. Though this review was planned only for less than an hour, it would take his entire week to prepare. He had few client escalations to attend to as well. In fact, one of them was already asking for the contact details of the new CEO. He was scared if any one of these clients reached out to Marshal with an escalation, the unit review would be more of damage control.

Satvik looked at the agenda again; for the first two items, he had some data from the last review. The last point on new digital strategy got him worried. He had difficulty in understanding the hype around digital, because he thought all his professional life he had worked on computer programs only and all that was digital.

"Isn't all software programming digital per se?" Satvik always struggled to comprehend the renewed discovery about digital.

"No, not at all, not all software programming that we do is digital, mobiles apps are digital, websites are not," Ajesh replied.

According to Satvik, it was still quite vague, and different people understood different things by digital. Satvik always found sessions on digital focus digressing – from mobile usage to social media adoption to big data analytics. For his own convenience, he had simplified this understanding as 'anything on mobile phone is digital', though he was mistaken a few times.

Satvik recalled the example that Marshal gave on 'ownership' and hoped somehow he could connect his digital story with that. But from what he could infer from his talk, Satvik and his team were one of those who were working on legacy technologies. When Marshal talked of transforming Creative Tech, it was people like Satvik and his team who required a paradigm shift, Satvik thought.

Presenting the summary of the team's work in a short conversation was a big challenge for Satvik.

"Will Marshal really appreciate that my team is the working horse behind smooth operations of many banks? Though they do not quite understand fancy terms like 'digital disruption', they know exactly how our software works and fixes it requires in time. When I motivate them by saying they are crucial for the smooth functioning of our economy, it is not an exaggeration."

"What if Marshal gets an impression that our team is not futuristic enough in thinking? Are we on the wrong side of his digital story? Will he encourage us or denounce our approach?"

Satvik was getting increasingly worried.

"Is there no way we can postpone this review for a later date?"

Satvik asked Vikas the first thing in the morning, almost pleading for a 'yes'. Satvik always hated unexpected work like this.

"Do you think I have an option of saying no? At the maximum, we can postpone it by few days, but we can't be seen dilly-dallying to the explicit ask of a new CEO," Vikas responded. Understandably, he was more tensed about this review than Satvik. This was the first opportunity for Vikas to strike the right rapport with Marshal – 'make or break'.

When Vikas would be tense, he would ask Satvik to accompany him for a cigarette break. As per a recently announced policy, the company had banned smoking in campus premises – one had to walk some distance to a designated corner. It was deliberately created to discourage people from smoking, but it had a contrary effect. The smoking corner was a good socializing place.

"Most of the crucial decisions get made during the smoking break," Vikas said.

"Now I understand why smokers grow faster in the organization," Satvik joked. "That's why I always accompany you during smoking breaks."

"We must come out well in this review with Marshal; there should not be any goof-ups," Vikas told Satvik.

"We don't have a choice; we have to impress him with our current work," Satvik responded as Vikas exhaled the smoke.

"See, Arvind, our last CEO, knew our work as he was a long timer in the company. I knew his line of thinking and we could adapt to the same. Last few reviews have been a cakewalk as we knew exactly how to present our case," Vikas said.

"True, but this also is an opportunity to get more budget and resources – something we have been struggling with Anand. Marshal is talking about growth and innovation." Satvik believed thinking positive results in a positive outcome during difficult times.

Vikas and Satvik spent several days trying to put the numbers together. They finally prepared a detailed presentation for Marshal. Satvik also collected the feedback from his other colleagues that Marshal had reviewed with earlier. Everyone said Marshal was very quick in coming to the point and asked the right questions. He preferred insights and visual display than raw numbers.

"Where are the actionable items?" Marshal had asked people in the other reviews. He encouraged them to think beyond the current limitations and gave targets for the next year. He was seen as a hard task master – a very important quality of a good leader.

Satvik somehow wanted to let the storm pass without much damage.

On Friday, both Vikas and Satvik went up to Marshal's room for the meeting. They also kept three key team members on stand by, just in case more details were required.

The CEO's office had a new secretary, Sherlyn. A middle-aged American lady, she was not new to Marshal.

"I have seen that when senior executives change companies, they also take their long serving secretaries along," Satvik commented.

"CEO's secretaries are sometimes more powerful that their bosses. We must strike a good rapport with her. I am sure Sherlyn knows Marshal well – his interests, likes, dislikes even the medicines that he takes and what would make his wife angry," replied Vikas.

"Rightly said. The last reason you mentioned, that itself is good enough for Marshal to retain Sherlyn, even if it came at a little bit of extra cost," Satvik responded.

Sherlyn greeted them with a broad smile and told them to wait in the adjoining room as Marshal was running late from the previous meeting. Satvik wished that Marshal got delayed further so that their review was shortened, or even better, cancelled.

The wait was especially grueling. Satvik asked Vikas, "A CEO's office can't manage the timing of their own meetings? They didn't even inform us that the meeting is delayed."

"I always plan my day. In the morning, before start of the work day, I plan all the activities for the day, write it on post-it chits and tick them off before leaving for the day. If I get delayed in any meeting, I send an advance apology or cancel the meeting beforehand."

"And possibly that's why you are not where Marshal is – a predicable job always brings limited returns," replied Vikas.

Satvik was not amused at Vikas's sarcasm. He thought Vikas was making fun of him. But that's how Vikas was – with some black humour, but good at heart. He was one of the fastest growing persons in the company. "I want to be the CEO of Creative Tech one day," Vikas would say often. He was not hesitant to take calculated risks and stand by his decisions – the sign of a good leader. Most importantly, Vikas offered much needed support to his team. The only thing that he was afraid of was heights; nothing else bothered him.

"What I meant was Marshal has a series of critical meetings and one delay gets relayed to the other, and then it becomes unpredictable," Vikas tried to soften the sarcasm in his previous sentence.

"True, he has lots of meetings planned, but he also has a battery of secretaries to manage the timings of those meetings. It was more a question of respecting the time and effort of your own colleagues," Satvik built further on his argument.

Though Vikas had been Satvik's manager, due to long working relations they had become good friends.

It was clear that they were not likely to conclude this debate there; just that it helped them in killing time and reducing a little bit of the anxiety. It reminded Satvik of the fearful viva-voce during school, and how difficult it was to wait till his turn came. The worst possible outcome could be that the meeting was postponed for the next day after waiting for a few hours.

Luckily, after two hours, Vikas and Satvik were called into Marshal's room.

Satvik had been to his CEO's office earlier. It was a spacious, well lit room, but he didn't recall anything significant. This time it looked quite different and very modern. There were bean bags along with sofas. The carpet was re-done to make it look like a five star hotel room. One of the walls was coloured beautifully and painted with different artworks. There was a collapsible glass board and multiple screens for video conferencing. A big TV screen was showing all the business news, though the sound was muted. "Wouldn't be a distraction for a busy day of the CEO with so much of multi-tasking already?" Satvik thought.

Marshal was an Apple fan, it appeared – all the gadgets in his room were interconnected Apple devices. Apple devices were usually not that common in the office, firstly due to cost consideration and secondly that they were not quite compatible with other devices. So the bunch of Apple tablets, laptops and iMacs looked more like an elite and disconnected ecosystem of their own. The CEO's office was refurbished specifically to the liking of the new incumbent.

Vikas started the presentation, first by giving a brief history of the unit, background of work they did and key initiatives done during the last few years. Marshal listened patiently for first ten minutes and then intervened.

"I have been observing this during my reviews of many units last few days – almost all the teams are bogged down by challenges of the past. If we don't break free from our historical background, we can't think radically to transform ourselves," Marshal said like a no-nonsense person.

It looked as if someone had slapped Vikas. He skipped all the slides of background and context. Satvik also made a mental note of not using the background or past challenges again in meetings with Marshal.

"Why is there a need to have such a large team to fix software defects and future upgrades? A good software should not have so many defects and it should improve itself over time. The effort should be to prevent the defects during coding itself and not to have a large team downstream to support it," Marshal commented next.

"Valid point," Satvik thought, just that on the ground things were quite different.

Marshal then spoke about the concept of 'ageless software' – an in-built intelligence in the code that can improve itself over time. He also spoke about the research that he had done in this area in his doctorate days.

The other focus area was automation.

"We should use standard tools available in the market to automate some of these support tasks. These days machine learning can be successfully deployed to automatically solve many repeat issues."

"Last year we deployed three tools to automate the support tasks. We have further optimized resources by having a centralized team, instead of having client specific teams. It was due to these efforts that the unit had been able to reduce the cost by 20% over the last one year," Vikas responded.

"We have not hired engineers since last two years, even the attrition cases were not filled," Satvik seconded Vikas in convincing Marshal how efficiently the team had been running their operations.

"That is really excellent, however I think there is opportunity for more. I have done a rough back of the envelop calculation and I believe that there is further possibility to make this team more lean and smart. We can release 40% of your current team from repetitive support work and deploy them in more value adding work. This can help generate 10 million USD additional revenue for us," Marshal was quite polite, but firm at the same time.

Marshal would take long pause in between sentences, but that only meant more finality in what he said. Marshal was tall, certainly above six feet in height. Though in his fifties, he could probably outrun Satvik and Vikas any given day. He commanded respect not only through his formal position as CEO, but his overbearing physical stature as well.

Satvik had seen in his meetings with the management team that while he mentioned the efficiency gain example as proof of his pro-active approach, it sometimes backfired. Instead of getting applause for the past improvement in efficiency, they got new targets to improve further. It was something like when you proudly tell someone that you just finished a 10 km marathon and the person replies – but why not 15 km, what went wrong? A clever management always converts the past achievements of the team as a proof-point for even steeper targets. Efficiency targets are the never-ending gold mines when it comes to assigning targets.

In hindsight, Satvik thought it could have been better to talk about problems like that they had failed to reduce team size in the past as the volume of work had increased many folds. But Satvik was not bold enough to say that to his new CEO, neither was Vikas.

"I want to bring a fundamental change in the mindset of all leaders. Today they think if they manage more people, they are more successful. We need more revenue, not more people," Marshal said.

"Socialist organizations measure success by number of people employed, the new age organizations like Creative Tech should be measured by revenue per person.

"If you are really interested to know how the new age companies work, google a small company called Vcoin in the valley. They are roughly around twenty-five people, two years old, but already talking of business opportunities in hundreds of millions. They have used bitcoin technology to create a successful product."

Satvik thought Marshal was right. It was still a mindset issue. He recalled how his father boasted that Tata employed a large number of people. Employment was a social welfare activity, wasn't it?

"Okay, where are we on the digital transformation? I see you have just one slide," Marshal asked.

Satvik and Vikas looked at each other's faces, one hoping the other to take the lead. This was already a weak link in their presentation. With the previous comments from Marshal, this seemed even worse.

"Marshal, this is an area we have not yet started working on. But I can assure you that this is at the top of our agenda. Since your address in the town hall, we have been thinking about the right approach to handle this," Vikas replied.

"We have sent five of our team members for the three-week training program on data science. I am also taking an online course," Satvik replied.

"Guys, we don't have time to think forever, we have to act fast. It should not require a CEO's review for your team to think about these things. I am surprised that leaders like you still don't show the right urgency."

Satvik heaved a sigh of relief, not because he sensed any kindness in those words, but because Marshal was looking at Vikas when he said those unflattering words. Vikas, on the other hand, took out a kerchief to wipe out few accumulated drops of sweat that appeared on his forehead.

It was a very long forty-five minutes for Satvik and Vikas. The colour on the wall looked faded that time and the bean bag that was so comfortable earlier started hurting in a way. Finally, the review ended with some action items.

"We should have protested when Marshal was talking about new targets," Satvik suggested to Vikas.

"In a situation like this," Vikas replied, "as middle managers, we have only two options – contest the target and get fired right away, or reluctantly accept the target and wait for a miracle to happen. One day everyone has to die, at least the second option gives us some time and don't forget that miracles do happen."

"But we know that we will not be able to meet that target."

"If we are able to find a convincing reason why the target could not be achieved, we can still manage the situation. That is called expectation management," Vikas replied.

"Marshal gave us a solid lecture on digital and still I am clueless on what to do about it. I could not even ask any questions," Satvik said.

"Good that you did not. Sometimes in corporate discussions, it is clever to act stupid as the other person gets an opportunity to showcase his knowledge and this helps reduce his anger."

Vikas and Satvik both hoped somehow Marshal should forget about this review, but such wishes never come true. They wished they had one more chance, now that they knew what Marshal was exactly looking for.

Vikas and Satvik were walking back to their office discussing what went wrong and how they could improve the next time when they received the mail from Marshal's office.

From: Marshal Scott
To: Vikas Raj; Satvik Saxena

Sub: New target for banking support unit

Vikas/Satvik,

Your banking support team is doing a commendable job, however there are significant opportunities for improvement, viz.

1. *Reduction of headcount by 40% by effective use of automation tools.*
2. *Increase of revenue by 10 MUSD during current year by providing value added services.*

Also, I look forward to more clear strategy on digital adoption soon, beyond training your team members and taking online courses. It is important for our transformation.

I will ask my office to set up a follow-up call next month.

Cheers,
M

Now Satvik realized where he had landed – a goal that seemed impossible to achieve. During such occasions, he thought he was lucky not to have been promoted. At least he was not in the first line of fire like Vikas.

Satvik was thinking that this was the biggest problem with leadership change that a middle management had to bear. Every time a new CEO came in, he completely disregarded the previous efforts on cost reduction, efficiency, revenue growth, etc. The clock restarted for him or her just like a clean canvas. He would set a new target of further optimization of an already optimized set up.

Later in the day, Satvik had a meeting with his team members. Some of them were curious to know what happened in their meeting with Marshal. Satvik almost felt scared to tell them that Vikas and he had got a new target on behalf of the team – and both of them had no idea about how to achieve it. At least Satvik's team would have demanded more reasoning from him on how they agreed to such an idiotic target. Some of his team members already had a very low opinion of managers – that they were not assertive enough to present the right picture of the challenges faced by the team. They believed that managers like Satvik were mere messengers of management decisions and actions.

Satvik told them about the digital challenges and opportunities that Marshal spoke to them about. He still did not tell them about the new target. It was awkward to reveal such a thing in the team meeting. Satvik had learnt with time, how to tell selective truths to the teams.

Over the last many years of working together, Satvik and Vikas had an unwritten understanding on their roles. Vikas would manage the senior stakeholders and Satvik would manage the team directly. It was Satvik's responsibility to align the team for the new target – a target that they did not choose and had no idea on how to implement. Satvik still thought Vikas's job was a lot harder than his. Vikas would be directly held accountable for those targets in the next follow-up meetings.

Satvik's experience of working in Creative Tech had taught him that as one moved up in seniority, the degree of freedom reduced to a large extent. While at the junior level, employees could still question, throw tantrums and vehemently disagree with their seniors, at the senior level, this option diminished greatly. Satvik's team could still question him on his decisions, Satvik could do slightly less with Vikas and finally Vikas had almost no option to question Marshal. At the senior level, people were paid a higher salary to comply and implement, not to ask unhelpful questions. The middle management employees like Satvik became the perennial punching bag during all such transitions.

Ajesh also had a similar review and his experience was no different. He also ended up taking a steep target, however he was good at maneuvering the digital conundrum. That guy knew all the acronyms like SMAC, GAFA, and what not – thanks to his addiction for LinkedIn, he came out in flying colours in his review.

"Marshal has selected me as one of the 'Digital Change Evangelists'," Ajesh told Satvik.

"What does that mean?"

"We will be a team of twenty-five key people who are expected to create right perception for the transformation mindset. We will be the legs on the ground for his initiatives. Marshal has set up a monthly review meeting with our team," replied Ajesh.

"Congratulations, Ajesh! It is really good to be in the good books of the CEO."

For Satvik, digital was a stick that he could be beaten with any given day. The sad part was that most of these conversations with Marshal were internal focused. There were limited discussions about the client value maximization which used to be the cherished goal for Creative Tech in the past.

Satvik took the last bus after the review late in the evening. The company bus always gave the pulse of the employee mood.

"I had lost hope on my promotion, I couldn't believe when I received my letter designating me as 'Senior Software Engineer' last week," one of the engineers in the front seat was telling his colleague.

"Even the 10% increments have been generous, considering that it was frozen for the last two years," his friend responded.

"I think we should all thank our new CEO for these changes. He has relaxed our work timings, introduced casual wear and even allowed Facebook browsing during work hours."

Satvik agreed with most of their observations, but the new target was playing at the back of his mind. He dozed off in the bus; for the few minutes he was asleep, he dreamt of achieving all that Marshal had said that day.

It was his twentieth work anniversary at Creative Tech. Satvik was being facilitated with the 'Best Employee Award'. He proudly looked at his family members sitting in the first row in the audience. His father waved at him, reminding Satvik of a similar function when he was awarded for the long service in his company. Marshal handed over the plaque to Satvik amidst huge applause in the auditorium.

At this time, Satvik felt a sudden jerk and the familiar noise of the door opening. His bus had stopped.

While walking up to his house, Satvik thought, "Will my dream really come true one day?"

"So when are we going to buy our new apartment?" Neeraja asked Satvik when he reached home.

"We will buy it soon honey. I must tell you about an interesting concept that our new CEO, Marshal shared with all of us."

"The media is going gaga about him; he seems to be a technology visionary," replied Neeraja.

"He said that soon people will stop owning things, they will only pay for the services that they use and the ownership concept was a passé. Why should we incur a heavy investment in that case and tie ourselves in knots."

"Your CEO might have fooled his employees, but don't try that on me."

"Does Marshal live in a rented apartment?" Neeraja asked further.

"No, I heard he owns a palatial house in a very upscale area in Palo Alto." Satvik realized that Marshal's vision had limited application when it came to dealing with Neeraja.

"I was looking at some of the advertisements of houses that will fit our budget, and soon we will buy one," replied Neeraja.

The CEO's Mantras
of Transformation

"I read the reports about you in the Indian media. Really amazing. I am really happy for you," Monica told Marshal.

"Yes, they have been very flattering."

"I spoke to the chairman last night. He has very high expectations from me. According to him, I am not hired to just manage the status quo, I am hired to engineer a big turnaround. The IT industry is undergoing disruption, so I am supposedly the change agent."

"First of all it is Chairperson, not Chairman." Monica always corrected Marshal whenever he forgot to use a gender neutral term, even in private conversation. According to her, subconscious biases like these were bigger reasons that women were still not empowered in society. She even objected to 'mankind' – the right word should be 'peoplekind'.

"Okay, I stand corrected, chairperson." Marshal always valued Monica's opinion – his wife, friend and counsel, all combined into one. She was working with one of the venture capitalists that invested in Silicon Valley startups.

"Honestly, I feel surprised at my initial discovery as a CEO. Though Creative Tech is a technology company, to me it resembles the manufacturing companies of the 80s. Possibly this company is running twenty years behind where it should be."

"I follow some of these IT services companies well – they are like sweat shops. Someone started a shop and the shop got bigger and bigger with time until it could no longer grow and the size itself became a problem," Monica agreed with Marshal.

"Yes, exactly. I heard a new term today 'linear growth' – it meant the only way to grow the revenue was by hiring more people and bill them to the client projects. These are called 'Time and Material (T&M) contracts'. It is a very dated concept and lacks innovative thinking," Marshal responded.

Being in the Silicon Valley, Marshal had seen many new age startups. They hardly had few hundred employees and some of them were already nearing billion dollar revenues. Creative Tech was on the other end of the spectrum. They had massive fifty thousand employees and the revenue per employee was miserably low.

Another thing that bothered him was the excessive focus on cost in almost everything. If Creative Tech was such a miser company, it would affect the productivity of the employees. If his own expenses were under microscope of thrift, he would almost certainly feel constrained. Creative thinking does require some kind of financial freedom. One can't throw peanuts and expect high value creative employees to be productive. The executives in American companies were well taken care of in perks and remunerations. This was another key difference between a value based company and cost based company.

Marshal's first real induction in the company was done by Rajendran, his deputy and the COO of the company. Rajendran was just a few years away from his retirement, but looked much older for his age.

"I feel privileged to get my induction done by the most tenured employee in Creative Tech," Marshal said.

"I take it as a compliment," Rajendran replied.

"Of course yes, retiring in an IT Company is unheard of. I have never attended a retirement function ever in previous software companies."

Rajendran accompanied Marshal for the campus tour, proudly showing some of the modern state-of-the-art glass structures. He explained in detail when each and every building came up and a brief story around it. There was a giant swimming pool and many fountains at various places. The company gym and recreational facilities could compete with the best in the world.

"This banyan tree that you see is five hundred years old," Rajendran pointed to a nearby tree.

"I am really impressed – the campus is so green," Marshal replied.

"Yes, we take care of all the energy needs of the campus through sustainable means. The campus generates its own energy requirements through solar panels,"

"That's really great. Tell me, what is the most unique thing about Creative Tech, Rajendran?" Marshal asked.

"Very difficult to answer," replied Rajendran, "but if you insist, it is the culture of this company. In spite of various ups and downs, the company has preserved its soul – its value system."

Initially Marshal tried to sincerely understand the culture and background of the organization. Though he was gaining insights, Marshal realized quickly that it was not a workable approach, it was like falling into quicksand. He often encountered a series of circular arguments that did not help reaching any conclusion. Creative Tech had a long history of excellent performance, barring the last few years when it started wobbling. There were many stories that Marshal learned – each of them were like complicated knots and that would never get resolved.

Any new idea that Marshal would give, someone in his executive management team would tell him "yes, this approach was tried in the past, but it did not work." Marshal would appear ignorant for suggesting a solution that was already proven to be a failure. He had no direct way to know what was tried and why that failed. Marshal suspected that his team was sometimes trying to outsmart him by giving excessive reference to past decisions. He had to quickly find a way out of it. Also, he realized that in order to develop team empathy, he was slowly becoming more like them in thinking and action.

"A transformation can't be triggered from inside out; it has to be outside in," Marshal told himself. "A leader must be dispassionate to the context, otherwise there was no need to hire someone like him for the CEO position."

This became the fundamental mantra for Marshal for all his future course of action. He interrupted his executives whenever he witnessed they were telling him all about past stories.

"I am not interested in folklores and history; for me they are only excuses," Marshal would say in these situations. Marshal made the first principle of transformation '**don't get entangled with history for future direction– especially when it comes to digital transformation**'.

Marshal had a long professional career and he had had challenging assignments, but nothing was like being the CEO of a struggling company looking for a turnaround. Everyone looked up to him for direction and clarity. He had two choices – either provide initial direction first and course correct later in case it went wrong, or do a thorough analysis before providing any direction. Increasingly, he realized that he just couldn't afford an analysis-paralysis syndrome.

He was expected to act fast. A wrong decision could be corrected later, but a delay in decision was more dangerous in the existing context.

A lack of direction was more detrimental than change of direction. Marshal adopted a choice of action over wait. Thus **'preference to act fast'** became his second mantra to deal with the prevailing situation. The last thing that an organization should be seen is battling indecision, something that Marshal thought was plaguing the previous management. He had seen the impact of some of the small decisions on the employee policies – it created so much of goodwill. Speed was the most important thing.

"Rajendran, to create momentum in the team, we need aspiration targets for everyone," Marshal told Rajendran.

"No doubt about it, we need to set at least a 25% higher target to meet the numbers," Rajendran replied.

"That is not enough. I tell you, complacency is the biggest reason that organizations fail. It is better to set a 2x target and underachieve it by 1.5x rather than setting a target of x and over achieving it by 1.25x," Marshal replied.

"Some people may get de-motivated if they feel they have no realistic chance to meet the target," Rajendran replied.

"There may be a small percentage of people like that, but think again Rajendran, do we really need those people?"

This became the third principle for Marshal **'Set Aspirational Targets'**. He wanted everyone in his company to dream, and dream big. Everyone should have a goal which was truly inspirational. If there was a possibility to err in goal setting, let that be on the higher side, Marshal thought.

Marshal also realized that unusual situations require extraordinary measures. If an organization needed a turnaround, it had to find the next big idea that was transformational. This meant a break from the current business practices in search for new products and services.

The world was moving towards digital, and Creative Tech could not afford to be left out. He had not been hired to *run* the business as a shopkeeper, but to *change* it as an entrepreneur of the future. He had to experiment with the big ideas. The organizational context was his laboratory. This formed the fourth tool of transformation – **'Look out for big ideas'.**

One of the reasons that organizations fail, Marshal thought, was because of their people. The same people who build the organization sometimes unknowingly become the reason for its failure. Things that worked in the past do not work in the future and some people do not unlearn fast enough. A CEO may not have all the time to convince everyone before initiating a change. Marshal needed people who could believe in him to execute his ideas. Though he encouraged people to question and critically analyze his suggestions, he believed that some people opposed change for the sake of it. He did not want to waste too much of his time only to convince his executives why a certain decision was required. Large corporations are run by few smart people, he believed.

Marshal remembered quickly some of the best and most trusted people he had worked with in his professional career in the past. He decided, may be it was time to get them back to work with him again. This was his fifth tool of transformation – **'build a network of trusted people'.**

Another reason that organizations die, is the lack of creativity and innovation among their employees. Every day, thousands of employees come to office, but very few apply their creative self in day to day work. Marshal once told his wife Monica, "You know why there is such heavy security at the entrance of Creative Tech?"

"It is because when thousands of employees enter the office daily they leave their brains at the gate, the heavy security is meant to guard them till the evening when the employees get them back."

Monica did not quite get the joke, however she did understand that Creative Tech was badly in need of some people in Silicon Valley. She had never been to India before Marshal took up this job, though she was impressed with her first visit to the Creative Tech office. Marshal would often share his thinking with her for a second opinion and validation.

"I want each and every employee to think out of the box, to change the way things worked," Marshal stated.

"In large organizations, the middle management generally lack spirit; the junior employees are more amenable to innovative approaches. You should directly try to connect with them," Monica suggested.

"Exactly, that was the reason behind my idea contest where I solicited response from each and every employee of the organization. There was tremendous response of the campaign. I have got 20,000 ideas."

'Innovation and Creativity' was the sixth mantra for Marshal.

These six principles became an effective tool for Marshal for setting the new vision of the company and implementing it. They were his ideological strength. As much as he believed in these tools, he also thought that most of his current executive team might not get them. For example, why would his current executive team ever believe that at least some of them had failed in leading the right way and hence their learning would be of little consequence for future success?

When Marshal shared these six principles with Monica, she remarked, "You are forgetting one very important factor – cultural change."

"Not at all. I know I have to eventually fix the culture of the organization; something that I believe is out of tune with the current context. It sometimes angers me when Rajendran passionately speaks of the company culture as past glory. I think what he describes as a solution is actually part of the problem," Marshal replied.

Monica said, "Exactly, it was the same problem that Kodak refused to see when digital photography was increasingly being adopted. It is not possible that Nokia being a leader in mobile phone market did not see the smartphone revolution. They would have seen that coming, just that some leader in the company would have blocked the change by giving the reference of past glory and culture of the organization."

"The fact is, it becomes very difficult to defocus from the present for the sake of a brighter future. It requires great conviction to steer the organization at such junctures. The change management is predominantly a leadership issue," replied Marshal.

"The way I see in this whole situation, you have to be like a doctor that has been engaged to treat a seriously ill patient. It is never going to be a smooth path. More often than not, the situation gets worse before improvements and final recovery. The pain is going to increase; the patient might even ask the doctor to stop. This, however, does not deter the doctor to operate on the ailing patient," Monica advised.

"If there is one thing that is in short supply, it is time. As for any new management, there is always something called a honeymoon period when everything looks good and no one asks any questions. If this period is not used well to prepare for the change, one fine day there will be a barrage of questions," Monica added further.

As a CEO, Marshal knew he had to act fast. He had to be a man in a hurry. With such clarity of thoughts, ready tools of transformation and clear anticipation of things to come, Marshal thought he was now ready to work on the plan that the Board had hired him for.

The stage for the big transformation of Creative Tech was set well.

Hitting the Ground

The quarterly results always created a festive buzz in the Creative Tech campus. There would be colourful OB vans of many media channels moving around, and sometimes reporters could be seen with their big mikes. Employees were strictly prohibited to even go near them. The media could interact with only authorized representatives. The media interest in Creative Tech had always been phenomenal, whether the company was doing good or bad.

This was the first quarterly result for Creative Tech after Marshal had joined as CEO. He was just three months into the company, so the media was not expecting any great outcome as such. However, they were interested to know the direction that the company had set for itself.

Marshal had flown down to India for the quarterly results. Creative Tech had a small marketing office in Silicon Valley, which acted more like a sales and marketing arm. However, since Marshal joined as CEO, this was the centre of most of the action. Marshal spent most of his time in this office and also expanded that to include more staff. Marshal took pride in saying that the new office of Creative Tech was just a few blocks away from Google and Facebook.

Before the result announcements, Marshal took a round of the campus in a self-driven golf cart, waving at the media personnel occasionally. He was making a statement of intent and direction.

'Creative Tech takes giant leap with focus on Artificial Intelligence and robotics' – one of the enthusiastic news channels put up as breaking news.

Marshal was very articulate at handling the media. He enjoyed this new-found attention as well.

"This self-driven cart is designed and developed by a small team of our employees as a test project; this was one of the ideas that I had received in the 'Ideathon'. This first model was created in only thirty days," Marshal told the reporters.

"This is no doubt an excellent beginning. We are curious to know how do you define the turnaround and how long do you think it will take for Creative Tech?" one of the reporters asked Marshal.

Marshal was well prepared for a question like that. He responded calmly, "For any transformation to succeed, a clear articulation of the goal is most important. First three months as the CEO of this organization, I have spent most of my time in doing exactly that. We have set three goals for Creative Tech for the next five years:

1. We will become a 10 billion USD company from the current 5 billion
2. 80% of our revenue will come from digital practice, from the current 10%
3. We will inculcate a culture of innovation and will be known for R&D and high value products and services

"First two are quantifiable goals, the third one is not. However, the third goal is the most crucial for the achievement of the first two. We recently conducted a company-wide idea contest and the results were overwhelming. We got 20,000 new ideas to work on. These ideas from the rank and file of the company will eventually transform Creative Tech."

The follow-up questions came, "The outsourcing organizations have been under disruption due to adoption of automation and efficiency tools, their growth rates have gone down to single digits. Do you really think in such an environment, it is possible to achieve a target like doubling your revenue?"

Marshal was quite confident in answering questions on digital disruption because he had repeated it so many times in the past, and he knew the answer like the back of his palm. He gave a detailed explanation of the 'ownership' example.

He added further, "What you mention as disruption is opportunity for us, automation is a tool for us to re-deploy our resources at high-value activities and artificial intelligence is an arm for us to amplify human potential by launching new products and services."

There were few more questions, Marshal overall enjoyed his first quarterly results experience for the attention he was getting. He appeared in several media interviews as someone who very well knew what he was talking about. Everyone was waiting to hear his new vision for the company. He was the ray of hope to transform it from a struggling IT outsourcing company to a new-age digital entity. *The Business Line* published a comprehensive report.

'Creative Tech sets a bold direction under new CEO'

With 10 billion USD target, Marshal has set a bold vision for Creative Tech. He is not bogged down by the slowdown in the IT outsourcing and has taken a giant step with this. The good thing is that unlike the previous CEOs of Creative Tech, Marshal comes with a fresh perspective and does not have the baggage

of the past underperformances of the company. The earlier
management commentary was always boring and pessimistic,
replete with description of challenging times ahead. Marshal
has brought in the much needed change. If a transformation is
ever possible, it is now and there does not seem a better person
than Marshal to lead it.

The new CEO has also announced the appointment of an
R&D head and a sales head in the US. Research and client
engagement are two most important functions that needed
immediate attention in Creative Tech and could possibly be the
biggest driver for the new digital business. Marshal has also
been able to attract great technology leaders, some of whom
have worked with him in the past.

Most employees in Creative Tech were happy with the positive
undertone of the coverage during the quarterly result. Though the
result by itself was not great, the key thing was, unlike earlier times,
there was optimism and positive energy. There was a new goal to talk
about, a new chance to revive and hopefully a new strategy to work
on. Marshal was infusing the same optimism that employees had felt
in the good old days earlier. The board had selected the right person,
everyone was convinced.

"Marshal has brought in a new energy in the organization," Ajesh
said in one of the lunch sessions.

"Yes, he surely has," Satvik replied. However, Satvik thought Ajesh
went a little overboard when it came to praising Marshal. Ajesh had
stayed in the US for a long time. He had also tried to get citizenship
before he had to return during the financial crisis.

"He has increased the salaries of most of his executives; this will
surely motivate the leadership team," Ajesh added.

"I think that could be to reduce the spotlight on his own sky high salary," Satvik responded.

"This is one of the cultural changes that Marshal is going to bring – be ready for it. The compensation will not be peanuts anymore for the right talents," Ajesh went on to explain Marshal's actions.

Marshal was anything but frugal when it came to his approach towards company work. He hired a battery of consultants and advisors to manage his time and meetings. Though the previous CEOs tried to be a role model by showing how they travelled in economy class airlines, Marshal did not hesitate to hire company chartered jets.

"If the chartered jet saves a CEO's time for more productive use for company work, well, a few thousand dollars should not matter," Ajesh said.

Most employees agreed that Creative Tech should loosen its purse strings a bit. After all, it was still a company making a very healthy profit margin.

Marshal was really hard-pressed for time, or so it seemed. Few times his management team would travel with him in his jet to effectively use the travel time for meetings. Even while coming from the airport in Bengaluru, which was a good two-three hours' drive during busy hours, some of the executives would wait at the airport and accompany him in the car and have the meetings. Occasionally, Marshal would also conduct business reviews during these short travels.

"This shows that Marshal is really committed to his work, and that he makes best use of even his travel time," Ajesh pointed out appreciatively.

Ajesh added, "The most important thing is that Marshal has done well to engage with the customers, especially the American clients. They can relate to him far better. I have heard that Marshal could well be instrumental in getting some of the largest deals that Creative Tech has ever got."

Marshal made a lot of changes in the sales and client delivery functions. He created a deal advisory team that focused on large IT projects. This team was directly monitored by Marshal's office. Things were looking positive, for a change. There was a special team created to work with startups in Silicon Valley. They also kept an eye on potential acquisition targets. Marshal always used to get insights from his wife Monica who was actively working in this area.

"If you really want to be the new age digital company, you will have to be like one of these startups. Since your organization is inflexible and monolithic, the best approach would be to buy a stake in some of them," Monica told Marshal.

"Creative Tech has been a highly profitable company. They have a lot of cash surplus generated so far. Unfortunately, they have been very conservative in acquiring new companies," Marshal explained.

"They are wasting their cash in that case. I will let you know some of the best companies that Creative Tech can put their money in. I can right away tell you that Vcoin could be a great investment for Creative Tech," Monica assured Marshal on this aspect.

"Bitcoin has an idea acceptance problem even in the Board – they say it is not legal. I have tried a few times already," Marshal said.

Business Target for the Team

An employee town hall was set up soon after the quarterly result. The overall mood of the company was very positive. One of the employees asked about the bonus payment.

"Marshal, our clients have received our new vision very positively. Even the media coverage has been quite good. However, the employees really would want to know if Creative Tech management has decided to increase the bonus payment this time?"

"We will make it 100% this quarter for everyone," Marshal replied.

There was huge applause from the employees. No one could ever recall the last time when everyone had got the entire bonus amount. The word 'everyone' was very important. There was no scope of any 'conditions apply' kind of subtext.

The CFO and the HR head on the stage looked at each other in surprise. It appeared that Marshal had said that impromptu; it was not part of the town hall agenda. It was a nice thing to do for the employees, however it had some financial implications and required planning. The HR head also looked worried – if everyone would be paid 100% bonus, what was the use of the appraisal process and performance-based payouts?

Since the CEO had committed that in the town hall, it had to be implemented. It was like sops that politicians offer to people to keep them happy. As is true with sops, they need to get the required budget by savings from some other expenses, but that was for a later day possibly. Today everyone was happy at the financial windfall.

Satvik and Vikas were more worried about their forthcoming reviews.

"Did you get any details about the new 10 billion target that Marshal mentioned in the interview?" Satvik asked Vikas.

"No, I was not aware of this target at the company level. I am even more worried about the impact of this target on our unit. From the interview, Marshal appears to be a top-down target driven guy. He will not accept no for an answer," Vikas responded.

Both of them knew that they were in trouble, if Marshal stuck to his previous target as was sent in the last email. They did not have much time to work on that. Plus, they had no idea on how to achieve a hypothetical target that was thrust upon them. Satvik wished that somehow Marshal would forget about the unit target, but his office never forgot such things. In a week's time, another business review was set up by Sherlyn by Marshal's office.

It was again a two-hour wait outside Marshal's office, but it was something they were prepared for, based on their last experience. There were no surprises in the meeting room as well, just that Marshal himself was sitting on the bean bag and looked more relaxed than the last time. The TV in the room was showing that Creative Tech shares had been going up in the last three months.

Unlike last time, Marshal was very direct during the review this time. He asked Vikas, "How are we tracking to the 10 million USD target that we agreed last time during our review?"

Vikas had two options – either to present a false picture and postpone the problem for a few more months till finance reported the actual number, or speak the truth. Vikas recalled his ethical management reporting lessons and responded, "Marshal, I don't think we can meet that target this time. I have thought through various options, they seem very difficult," replied Vikas.

"But we agreed on it in our last review. The minutes of our meeting also mention that. If you really thought that the target was not correct, you should have replied immediately rather than coming up with a late excuse now," Marshal grilled Vikas further.

"Do you think you ever gave us a millisecond to react to your target last time? You forced the imaginary target on us without even understanding the kind of work we do or checking if that was realistic," Satvik felt like shooting back in the same tone. However, years of corporate mannerism had taught him to be more patient.

"No Marshal, I did not mean that," Vikas responded.

'Did not mean' used to be a last resort response, when Vikas had no idea how to defend himself and to react to situation.

"I don't like people who don't mean what they say or who don't say what they mean. We need competent leaders who can commit to the company targets and achieve them. We have wasted too much time in deliberation earlier," Marshal was becoming more aggressive.

This effectively shut the door for any further meaningful conversation. There was little scope of any recovery for Vikas and Satvik from here. They had only one option left – listen unquestioningly till Marshal chose to speak before leaving the room.

Satvik looked at his boss's face. Vikas just received a severe dressing down from the newly appointed CEO. For the first time, a confident and assertive Vikas looked vulnerable and worried. Vikas was damned if he spoke the truth and damned if he hid it. Without arguing further with Marshal, Vikas agreed to work on the revised number and promised to come back soon.

"What will we do now? Marshal is not going to listen to any excuse?" Satvik asked Vikas.

"He has already drawn up the plan based on the last target he gave us. That is how he came up with the 10 billion target for the company; he is not going to back down. Maybe, I should not have confronted him," Vikas thought in the hindsight.

Marshal, however, was less amused. He realized that if he wanted to turnaround the company, he had to show less tolerance for people who did not act proactively in time. Arguments and disagreements were alright, but when they started slowing down the swift execution of the company strategy, it was no longer helpful. Marshal looked up to his principles of transformation and concluded this was the time to act; he had to send the right messages.

Satvik wondered why people at the leadership level sometimes feel so powerful that any dissent is taken as refusal. Ironically, some of these people also grow quite senior in the corporate set up. Their continued success adds further to the self-aggrandizing behaviour to the extent that some of them become increasingly autocratic. Satvik thought Marshal was being unreasonable. He wanted a miracle out of them. On the other hand, Marshal had the bigger picture. He was there to turnaround the company, while Satvik was looking at the whole situation from his own prism.

Satvik got an e-mail that his reporting had been changed to a new manager named Robert, recently hired in the US office. When Satvik looked at Robert's LinkedIn profile, he understood Robert had earlier worked with Marshal in his previous organization.

"Was it that Marshal just wanted to remove someone from Creative Tech so that he could fill the position up with known faces?" Satvik could never know the answer to such a suspicion, he thought.

Satvik spoke to Ajesh about the review, "At our level, it is quite easy to sideline people without actually making it look like that. There are various ways to do it – one of them could be to just strip the person of any formal portfolio and keep him hanging in the system for some time without any explicit goal or targets. During the next appraisal time, the person could be tagged as not meeting company expectations with regards to performance.

"There are even harsher ways," replied Ajesh, "like making him report to his own junior or transferring him to some failed project which has no hope of recovery."

Marshal sent a mail introducing Robert to Satvik and his team, describing Robert's illustrious background and also the fact that they already had discussion and agreement about the new target. Satvik was even more amused about how a newly hired leader, without knowing the details of the business, would sign-up to a target? Satvik was more worried, knowing that the next failure to meet the target would be attributed to him. Robert would get away during the first few cycles, being new to the organization. A new hire always gets a longer rope in the organization for two reasons – one that they are seen as bringing the much-needed fresh perspective-and secondly, they are not seen responsible for the trouble that the company was already into. The companies follow a first-in-first-out under these circumstances.

Though Satvik was worried about his new boss, he was even more worried about Vikas. Vikas was not given any specific task and his old responsibilities were already transitioned to Robert.

Four weeks after this transition, Vikas got a meeting invite from Sujith – the HR head. As per established practice, the HR used to intervene in such cases and counsel employees. The meeting was set up in the corporate block – a very unusual place. The subject of the invite did not say much – it could be for some new assignments or future directions, Vikas thought.

Vikas arrived for the meeting well in advance. Dot on time, Sujith entered the room. Sujith had interacted with Vikas many times earlier; he had always been a nice, approachable person like all good HR leaders. After initial pleasantries, he asked Vikas if he was carrying his cellphone.

"I always keep my cellphone in a no-disturb mode during meetings. I know it could be irritating to others," Vikas replied.

"There have been a few instances when the employees have recorded confidential conversations and made it public in the media. We just do this as a practice for some meetings," Sujith replied.

At this point Vikas realized, this was not an ordinary meeting. However, Vikas had no other option but to hand over the cellphone. He was not on a strong standing anyway.

Sujith took out a piece of paper from his file and started reading.

"Mr Vikas, as you know we just completed our appraisal exercise in Creative Tech. We are a performance-driven organization and regularly promote employees for higher responsibilities. As part of the same exercise, we also find some employees, who we think we are not able to make best use of, for various reasons. This is not a commentary on the employee's capability, just that we may not have the right job matching their skill sets. I am sorry to inform you that you have been marked in later category in the last cycle."

"What does that mean?" Vikas could not believe what he had heard. He knew very well what an ominous note like this meant in the corporate world, just that he could not accept it was happening to him.

Sujith put the paper back in the file and said in a firm tone, "You will have to leave Creative Tech. Here is your resignation letter, you have to sign it here, below your name," he pointed with his finger.

The letter said that Vikas was leaving Creative Tech out of his own volition. A small footnote mentioned that he was being offered three months basic salary as compensation.

"What if I don't sign this letter? If I refuse to resign?" Vikas said.

"Then Creative Tech can terminate you for underperformance," Sujith showed him another pre-signed letter from the company HR. "In that case you may lose out on future employment opportunities because our experience letter would explicitly mention 'underperformance'. You may not get any compensation as well."

Vikas realized that he had very little bargaining power when it came to negotiating with Creative Tech as an organization. There was no point in arguing; it was a lost case.

"Okay, how much time do I have to think over it? Can I get back in a week's time?" Vikas pleaded.

"Ten minutes, or you may take fifteen if you wish, we have to complete this transaction in this meeting itself; it is a corporate guideline in such matters."

Sujith never looked so cruel; maybe he was just doing his job professionally.

Vikas signed his own resignation letter, the was lesser of the evil offered to him that time.

"Give me back my cellphone now," Vikas said.

At this point, Sujith called the company security, gave him the cellphone and instructed him to escort Vikas till the campus gate before handing over his cellphone back to him.

"Let me go back to my cubicle and collect my personal stuff," Vikas asked.

"Your company ID has been deactivated already, you will not be able to go back to the office building. We will have a security person deliver all your personal stuff to you at the campus gate. The laptop will be retained by us as it is supposed to be for office use only".

Vikas did not even get an opportunity to visit his cubicle one last time. He had a vague inkling about that when he had left for the meeting in the morning, but he did not know it could be so abrupt.

By 10 a.m., Vikas was outside the company gate and all his association with the company was over; it had just taken 45 minutes.

Vikas sat in his car. There was no laptop to be kept in the back seat. He had got back his uneaten lunch box. It was a very unusual return from office that day. The car did not start in the first attempt, Vikas pressed the key a second and then third time. Finally, when it started, Vikas zoomed off from the parking lot, saving himself the embarrassment from people who were still coming to office and finding space to park their car.

Vikas left the office, but a few minutes later, he stopped the car on the roadside. He couldn't go home. What would he tell his wife Shalini? He himself could not believe the sudden turn of events that morning, how would anyone else accept them. He needed time to convince himself of the new reality.

Vikas quietly left Creative Tech, a place that he called his home for seventeen long years. He did not even meet his team members or colleagues before he left. In the past, he had attended the farewell of many of his colleagues. It always used to be an emotional affair. Vikas never knew he would have such an inglorious exit one day that he would not even get a farewell.

Vikas was also worried about his future now. What would he tell his wife, his parents and friends? How would he explain the sudden exit from Creative Tech? Was it not shameful to admit that he was removed due to so-called underperformance? This sense of shame was hurting him far more than the financial responsibilities of EMIs and his kid's education.

Vikas's exit had an adverse effect on Satvik and his team members. As everyone came to know the way Vikas was removed, it left a bad taste and created a sense of fear in everyone's mind. If a senior person like Vikas could be removed like this, probably no one's job was safe. Moreover, people did not agree how suddenly after seventeen years of working in the same organization, one fine day an employee like Vikas could become a bad performer. Creative Tech was still making healthy profit; the growth had slowed down, but in no way was it a crisis situation.

"What was the need to remove Vikas?" Satvik asked Ajesh, "He could have been deployed elsewhere, even if Marshal was not happy with his current work. The least he could have done is, giving him sufficient time of at least three months to find another job."

Ajesh's response was based on his experience of such transitions in the past. He said, "Marshal has been brought to bring change and any large-scale change faces resistance from employees. He needs everyone to follow his vision and act swiftly according to his directions. Fear is a motivator at times to get things done. It hurts in the long term, but in short term, it creates an impression that the change is underway.

"Moreover, there is no ideal way to fire any employee. In most cases, the organization removes the person at a very short notice of a day or two. You can't tell a person about his firing and allow him to hang around for three months so that he will interact with other colleagues and spread negativity in the system. This may seem inhuman, but that is an acceptable practice in US when someone is laid-off. The process is cut and dry," Ajesh said matter of factly.

Satvik was not convinced at all. What happens to the long cherished culture of employee welfare and the ethical treatment of people? If employees felt afraid, they would never give their best performance. Positive environment is a bigger motivating force than fear. This was one thing that Satvik felt was the bad part of American corporate culture that was slowly seeping into Creative Tech. The CEOs sometimes got greedy and felt entitled to use short term measures like employee layoffs to manage quarterly targets. While they ruthlessly removed junior employees as excess fat, they added part of the savings to their own emoluments. This was a marked departure from the corporate culture that Creative Tech had built over a period of time. Satvik feared that Marshal was creating a bigger crisis in order to solve the current crisis.

Next day, in their team meeting, Raman asked about Vikas.

"Is it true that Vikas has been fired and he has left Creative Tech?"

"No, he has resigned and has left due to personal reasons."

Satvik had received a note from the HR on how to respond to his team on this matter. Satvik was expected to follow that strictly.

This was a façade that all employees have to live with as obedient corporate citizens. Although everyone knew that Vikas was fired, publically no one would utter a word. Under normal circumstances, when an employee left an organization after long tenure, there used to be a farewell for sure. If there was a silent exit, it surely meant something was wrong.

The New Manager

For Satvik, his work life had changed a lot since he was assigned the new manager – Robert based in Palo Alto. One of the biggest inconveniences was the new awkward work timing. Earlier Satvik could just walk into Vikas's cabin and discuss things to resolve them quickly. Now it was more of a 12-hour lag and Satvik had to work at odd hours. His effective work hours increased – Satvik had to be in the office for the day-job and later for catch-up with Robert late night on key issues and decisions. Satvik often thought of discussing this topic of extended work hours with Robert, but he was not quite sure how Robert would respond to that. Given the prevailing circumstances and stress in the system, Satvik decided to live with it and change his lifestyle accordingly.

"I think you should visit India for a few weeks, you can meet our team members and some of our key clients," Satvik had suggested to Robert during one of the catch-up calls.

"Yes, even I wanted to have my induction in India, but the thought of a fourteen-hour flight pulls me down. Moreover, I have some personal obligation, so travelling at this time will be difficult. As for the team, I think you are doing a great job in managing them," Robert said.

"I and Marshal had a chat yesterday. He said my immediate priority should be to set up a small team here. I plan to hire a few programmers, primarily in the new technology area. We need more local presence in US to drive our business."

"This is a good idea. How many people do you want to hire?"

"Something like ten to start with."

"I hope you have got the budget approval from Marshal."

"Marshal told me that he already had a discussion with you about this earlier. Our current team in India can be optimized by 30% that makes a business case for approximately ten hires in the US," Robert replied.

Satvik had totally forgotten about the target given by Marshal. He thought it had already taken one toll of Vikas, so he was fine. It seemed that Marshal still wanted Satvik to meet those targets. Now he understood why Robert desisted from developing any connect with the team in India. In absence of any personal understanding, for Robert, his team members only corresponded to a row in a large excel sheet; it was easier to fire that way.

"I am working on the team optimization, Robert, my view is that these people can be used in creating new digital projects with our existing clients. With that we can generate higher revenue, at the same time minimize any direct client impact," Satvik replied.

"No, let us release the team members to some other business units. Our net headcount should come down, that is what we have agreed with Marshal," Robert was very clear about what he wanted.

In many ways, Satvik realized Robert was a miniature version of Marshal. Robert was well aware that the only way he derived power in the organization was from his proximity with Marshal. He guarded that power line very well. After Robert joined Creative Tech, Satvik's communication link with Marshal was completely broken. Since Satvik was unsure of the communication between Marshal and Robert, he became even more careful in sharing things with Robert that Satvik feared could be problematic. So slowly they grew into a relationship where none of them trusted each other. This was an example of how open communication is the first thing that gets impacted in any large scale leadership change.

Meanwhile Marshal also expanded the innovation team in the US. He hired some of the most sought after techies from companies like Google, Facebook and Amazon. The newspapers reported them as 'trophy hires', more for their million-dollar salaries rather than the technology credentials they held. While the overall reporting was positive, some media reports also criticized the exorbitant salaries paid to them without assessing the corresponding value that they brought in.

When one of the reporters asked Marshal to comment on this, his response was, "If we need to hire the sought after techies from the valley, we will have to loosen the purse strings. Star programmers do not come cheap, after all. This is part of the cultural transformation which I believe has to precede the digital transformation."

The new hires in US could not be subjected to the same set of policies as was prevalent in Creative Tech, which was anyway dated. They had to be offered extra incentives, even to come onboard. They were given higher compensation, ESOPs and several other perks. To streamline things, Marshal hired a new head of HR for all hiring in US. This eliminated the unnecessary approvals required from a centralized system in India. He created a new set of policies in line with Silicon Valley companies. Marshal called it 'One company – two systems' to fulfill the need of the hour.

"Creating a specific innovation department is the sure shot way to undermine innovation in any company. Though it gives a bragging point to the CEO, it eventually discourages innovation by limiting the application to a few set of people," Satvik told Ajesh.

"There are alternate views as well. Have you heard of the story of PARC?" Ajesh told Satvik.

"Perhaps it is one of the most talked about and fascinating stories in the history of computers. In 1971, Xerox set up PARC (Palo Alto Research Centre) in the heart of Silicon Valley, hired some of the best talents of that time, provided them with ample fund and unlimited freedom with a small brief – to create an office of the future. Xerox was worried about the paperless office of the future with next generation computers.

"Over the next five years, what this team in PARC achieved was nothing short of phenomenal. They invented GUI (graphical user interface), Object oriented programming, Ethernet, laser printing, peer to peer & client server computing, personal computers and bitmap displays. They also contributed significantly to the development of internet. These inventions have generated wealth worth trillions of dollars."

"You are right about the story of PARC. However, that also explains why sequestering the new team from the corporate set up is not the best approach," Satvik tried to provide an alternate perspective.

He added, "Tim Brown in his book *Change by Design* talks about the politics of new ideas – most of the inventions in organizations fail not because the market rejects them, but because they are unable to navigate through the treacherous waters of the corporate set up. It gets even more difficult if the new idea is created by a set of new people in an isolated set up. It creates an 'us vs them' to make the adoption of invention even more difficult. While Xerox had little appreciation of what researchers at PARC did, the researchers themselves had lot of disdain for the bureaucratic set up of Xerox."

Both Satvik and Ajesh made valid points, but could not convince each other, and one more time, agreed to disagree.

Though the innovation team set up in the US got positive media coverage, it had a very different effect on Satvik's team. He could not explain why a similar team was not set up in India and why their team members were excluded from the new initiatives.

One day Radhika, one of the senior engineers in the team, came to Satvik's cubicle with a detailed calculation.

"Every single person hired in the innovation team in the US could be as costly as four people in our team. Does it mean that each of them add as much value that four of us combined can't do here in India?" Radhika asked Satvik.

"No, not all. I can say, each one of you add tremendous value through your work," Satvik responded, thinking the biggest affront to a software worker is saying that his or her work was not innovative. After all, as a manager, Satvik was equally responsible for the nature of the work his team was engaged in.

And Satvik did not need those calculations. He himself used to do similar calculations to demonstrate cost savings to American banks – this was a no brainer. He was at a loss to explain rationally to his team and he often took refuge in jargon like disruptive, digital, etc., to avoid directly answering these questions.

There was another side-effect of the US hiring on Satvik's current team. For many years, travelling to the US was one of the biggest motivators for the junior team members, what they commonly called 'onsite opportunities'. This was the elusive motivator that worked well when all other factors like salary hikes, promotion, etc., failed. The 'onsite' was the biggest hope, like a lottery for the software engineers. For many of the young engineers in IT, it was a dream to work and eventually settle in the US. With Creative Tech hiring more employees locally, it was no longer sensible to aspire for the American Dream. Satvik also stopped using 'onsite' as a carrot as far as possible.

Though Marshal's intent could not be doubted, his inadvertent actions were splitting the organization right from the middle – those who had worked long years in Creative Tech somehow were seen as the old economy workforce who needed significant overhaul and rework. They signified all that was wrong with the current organization that needed to be fixed. Incidentally, all of them were based in India. The newer set of programmers who were hired in US, were in the area of digital innovation – new technologies that according to Marshal was the hope for the future. This team had no baggage; they were in the investment mode. Incidentally, most of them also came at a much higher salary. This new team was least bothered about adjusting to the prevailing organizational culture.

The organization that Marshal inherited was unknowingly dividing itself into two warring factions that had more conflicts than alignments. This was unfortunate as it was happening at a time when Marshal needed complete alignment within internal teams to ride the turbulent sea of digital disruption.

This cultural clash was not only getting intense in the internal working of the team, but also slowly started impacting the future priorities and market focus. Earlier, the discussions around which market to focus for future products were more objective and less emotional. Now, increasingly, they were opportunities in 'my country vs your country' type of arguments.

"While focusing on the US is desirable, we should not lose our sight from the Indian market. It is opening up suddenly for many digital innovations. With billion plus people, it could be the next growth option for Creative Tech," Satvik tried to convince Robert.

"But there are challenges in that market, it is very low value. Creative Tech has not been able to generate good business from India. Instead, Creative Tech should create a product for US markets and align the teams accordingly," was the expected response from Robert.

This discussion for Satvik was exhausting, as he had to eventually agree with Robert's view. Beyond a point, Satvik did not want to alienate Robert and meet the same fate as Vikas did. The organizational nucleus was slowly being shifted to the US from India and this itself was one of the biggest disruptions that was underway in Creative Tech.

Satvik was more circumspect in his transactions with Robert and Marshal. The sudden exit of Vikas had created a fear in Satvik that alignment to the leadership was more important. Vikas was too blatant in expressing that the revenue expectations from Marshal were unrealistic. Marshal took it more as a refusal to get along with the new change objectives. Marshal saw Vikas as someone who questioned and resisted the change. This incident made Satvik cautious about what he spoke and communicated officially. "The blunt honesty could be costly. I need to be politically correct," Satvik thought.

Satvik realized his own professional behaviour was changing fast in a very short time. He started saying what he believed would make Robert and Marshal happy. Even though he got upset with some of their decisions at times, Satvik learned how to diplomatically circumvent them. It was not only a clash of culture in the larger sense, his inherent personality was also getting split in what he felt and what he finally expressed. Satvik realized that he no longer could trust his managers for a risk-free exchange of ideas.

Satvik was convinced now, most of the large organizations were like political entity. There were conflicting priorities at play, different people saw things differently and there were power plays among them. Very quickly they devolve into various camps and everyone needs to be aligned to some camp for his or her own well-being and survival. This behaviour was camouflaged as 'alignment'. These alignments were also dynamic – the camps change, so do camp leaders. So it was very important to be vigilant.

Satvik realized that all managers eventually started politicking for their own survival. Creative Tech was never an organization like this, but when trust breaks, insecurity increases and unproductive behaviour takes centre stage.

Crisis Management

The year-end used to be a hectic affair for Satvik and his team. While everyone around would be planning parties and celebrations, Satvik and his team would be on standby for the successful run of the critical processes of the bank. Something would invariably go wrong in some bank and this would create panic at times. This team at Creative Tech was in the same category as the traffic cops who would be busy monitoring the partying revellers on the festival days.

On earlier occasions, Vikas would be sitting at the bank's IT centres in Mumbai, while his team would be providing support at their Bengaluru office command centre. It was never a smooth day, and Satvik somehow used to survive it. This time, there was no Vikas. Satvik explained this to Robert and asked him to come to India and perform a similar role that Vikas used to do.

"A senior manager from our team generally helps in coordinating well and manage the crisis, if any," Satvik told Robert.

"But why should there be any crisis for a regular affair like this?"

"I don't know, Robert, but for the last many years, I have seen that something or the other goes wrong. It is not only us, sometimes the mistakes happen from the bank's IT operations as well. As a vendor, we always get called out."

"You need to plan it well; you are fully empowered to take decisions."

In corporate world, a sentence with words like 'fully empowered' indirectly means that the manager is washing his hands off this and the person will be solely responsible for managing the crisis. There is little that one can do if it comes from one's own boss.

On the eve of 31st December, Satvik would buy a lot of food and soft drinks for the team for overnight office stay. This was the small incentive for the team members who always cursed Satvik for calling them on such occasions. He used to apply all the tenets of team management during this period. He would also play the radio, just to create a celebratory atmosphere. This music had another purpose – to stop people from falling asleep during the wee hours.

Satvik used to paste a big chart on the wall with the names of the banks and the status of computer programs. Every hour, one of the team members would mark the successful completion of the activity. Any red cross meant that the program had halted and it needed quick intervention. The product engineering team used to step in at such occurrences. This set up was somewhat inspired by military command centre procedures during their critical operations. One of the prior program managers had worked in the army earlier, who had implemented this method in the team. It really worked well.

For the first three hours before midnight, things were running smoothly for most of the banks. Satvik was relieved to see so many green ticks on the chart. It denoted that everything was in order, however, until the branches opened the next day on time, the danger was not over. It was just a matter of a few more hours, and Satvik hoped this ordeal would be over.

"Satvik, one of the banks is reporting that their computer screen has frozen while running year-end operations. It has been like that since the last three hours," Raman came running to inform Satvik.

Satvik called up the data centre of the bank. "Can you check the application log from the system?"

"The system is not allowing anyone to login. It throws out giving some weird error."

"The system has been hanging for the last three hours, why did you not report it earlier?" Satvik was a bit worried that they may have little time to complete the remaining activities before the branch opened the next day.

"We thought the system was slow this time."

"Okay, Raman and Radhika – look into the error file for the time being."

"It is a very generic error – unauthorized access. We can't make out anything from this."

Satvik was getting increasingly worried with the situation. Slowly, more banks started reporting that error. In a period of one hour, 10 different banks reported the same error. The progress chart was all full of red crosses. The team mates were clueless as the command centre phone kept ringing incessantly.

"Someone please switch off that FM radio," said Satvik.

Satvik was so pre-occupied with the situation that he forgot where he had left his cellphone. Satvik needed to update Robert, just in case of any escalation from the banks, which was looking very likely by then. When Satvik finally found his phone, it had five missed calls from Marshal. Satvik feared that now he could be in real trouble.

Meanwhile, Robert called Satvik to check what had happened. Since Satvik did not respond to Marshal's calls, Marshal had called Robert and blasted him. Now it was Robert's turn to do the same to Satvik.

Satvik tried to explain the prevailing situation and the effort the team was making to solve the problem.

"I need a report in the next fifteen minutes."

This was always the catch-22 situation in a crisis. While on one hand there was a problem to be resolved for the clients, the senior managers kept asking for reports. Everyone in the hierarchy wanted to be updated of what was happening on the ground, more so if the manager was in a different location and was little aware of the context.

Satvik had to focus his energy on the problem resolution for the time being. It was already midnight and the bank users were not able to run the year-end programs. It could be disastrous if it continued in this way.

"We need more details to locate this issue. It is possibly a code issue. Let us get our product engineering team to look into this. Let us also get the audit log from the banks."

"Is there any pattern among the programs that are throwing this error?" Satvik asked Raman.

"It is such a generic error and is interrupting all the programs by forced log outs. Even the batch programs have stopped," Raman replied.

Satvik needed to make sure that the team did not panic. During crisis time, the team needed more support and empathy, Satvik thought. While he was getting blasted from Robert, Satvik was making sure that the team on the ground was in the best frame of mind.

"Hang on, since when have the banks started reporting this problem?"

"Around midnight?"

"And how many of the banks are reporting this problem now?"

"Well, 22 out of 45 banks have reported this problem. The remaining 23 are running their operations smoothly," replied one of Satvik's team members.

"It has got something to do with the time. Let us look in our code."

During times of crises, human brains either go numb or become super-efficient. Satvik could sense that in his team, while some did not know what to do, some of them would become very active. Raman was one such engineer, who always solved things in such situations.

"I have found the issue. There is a licence file that needed to be refreshed," after one hour of sifting through the code Raman said.

"Oh, such a silly thing. Thank god we finally found it."

It was a small oversight, but had a huge impact. In a normal situation, it would have been a routine affair, the bank would have procured the requisite licence and got the file updated in time; it was Satvik's responsibility to check that as well.

By the time they fixed the problems in the different banks, it was already 10 a.m. Some branches had to wait for at least one hour and the bank officers had to face the ire of their customers. It was not a pleasant situation, but Satvik was relieved that it was finally over.

While the problems for the clients were technically resolved with some noise, the repercussion of this incident internally was yet to be faced. Satvik and the team were exhausted, having worked for the last eighteen hours when Robert wanted to address the team before leaving the office.

"This was such a stupid mistake. You and your team should have pre-empted it."

"Robert, this is a shared responsibility with banks. It is not entirely our mistake. The team has done well to fix it well in time," Satvik responded.

"Do you know the damage it has done to our reputation? Marshal has been called by the regulator to explain why the banks should not impose a penalty on us. You and your team should be ashamed of this."

Satvik had never heard such words from his manager, that too in front of his team members. The role of a manager was also to defend his team in a crisis situation and not just blame them. Here, Robert had abrogated his own responsibility instead of shouldering it. Satvik thought – it is true that leadership characteristics do not get built during crises, they just reveal themselves.

"Okay, this incident had some learning for us. We will make sure that we do a root cause analysis of the events so that it is never repeated in the future," Satvik tried to calm Robert down who sounded agitated on the phone.

"I have spoken to Marshal. He says we need to take strict action."

"What do you mean by strict action?"

"The heads must roll. In the next twenty-four hours, I need the name of the person who had made the mistake in the licence file. In case you can't find who from your team is responsible, be ready with your own resignation letter." Robert became even more aggressive.

"Look at the audacity! First of all, Robert should have felt guilty for not being at the client site during the hours of crisis. Secondly, he should have supported his team and provided help. Instead, he was trying to act smart by blaming his own team who tried to salvage the situation," thought Satvik.

Satvik realized Robert was only trying to cover himself. When Marshal would ask Robert the next day – he would promptly respond that he had done a thorough review of the situation and removed the person responsible for the mistake.

It was not the right occasion to argue. Satvik left the room and asked the team members to go home and rest. He thought, let him sleep over the problem, and by morning Robert's anger would hopefully come down.

The next morning, Satvik met Ajesh and explained the series of events.

"I will call up Marshal and tell him the entire story. If there is one person who needs to be fired, it should be Robert."

"Are you mad? Do you think Marshal will believe you?"

"Why not? I had asked Robert to come to India and be at the bank data centres during this time, the way Vikas used to. But he refused. I think he is completely useless. Marshal should fire him."

"As a soldier, if you go to your Army General during a war and tell him that his most trusted lieutenant is useless, what reaction would you expect?"

"So, what should I do now?" Satvik asked Ajesh.

"Just go and tell Robert that you have found the person who wrote the erroneous piece of code that averted the pre-warning of licence expiry."

"But he said he would fire that person."

"That's fine. Just tell him that the code was written by Vikas."

"What if Robert checks it himself, and finds out I am lying?"

"He will not bother to check. He just wants to prove to Marshal that he has taken appropriate action," Ajesh said.

"It is not right. Vikas has been my best counsel and friend. He had always supported our team during difficult times. It will be like betraying him."

"It is your choice. We have to make difficult decisions at times when all the options seem wrong. We just pick what is less wrong and more prudent."

"We lie so many times in our daily lives in a corporate set up, this is still a benevolent lie – to protect someone in the current team by falsely accusing someone who is already presumed guilty," replied Satvik.

Satvik saved himself and his team members this time, but his bigger worry was what would happen the next time? The nature of work was such that client escalations could never be avoided. Was he supposed to live under the hanging sword all the time?

"I will have to fight back," Satvik thought. "I will meet Rajendran and find a way to deal with Robert."

CEO's Act 1

This was the 4th quarterly result since Marshal was hired as the CEO of Creative Tech. That marked the completion of one year for Marshal. Though Marshal had created the right vibes of change management and digital transformation, he could not arrest the fall in the quarterly growth. This time the company had lagged behind its peers in the growth rate. Creative Tech was still making healthy profits, but the media was more direct this time during the briefing sessions.

"Marshal, do you agree that your five-year target has been too lofty? Are you on the right track to achieve 10 billion in another four years?" One of the reporters asked him.

Marshal hesitated in the start then responded, "We are very much on to achieve the target. We have spent the first year in building the foundation for a big transformation. Creative Tech has now created a culture of innovation in the organization."

Marshal highlighted the innovation team that he had set up in the US, also mentioned that half of the organization had been trained in digital technologies. He brought attention to the key management positions that he had created and filled in the last year, some of them being – Chief Digital Officer, Chief Design Officer, Chief Architect, Chief Technology Officer and Chief Innovation Officer.

These roles in the corporate world were also called CxO roles, which started with Chief and ended with an Officer. The middle term was a variable that added to the fancy.

Satvik found these answers evasive. At least, he as a member of the middle management had no clue what Marshal was talking about. Though Marshal had hired key people in some newly created roles, it was not clear how these new CxOs would connect with the rest of the organization and drive change. One of the roles that Marshal created was called 'Chief Communication Officer' – Satvik found that rather amusing. The person was a senior vice president hired in the US who was responsible for all employee communication. Weren't things like communication management to be performed by each and every employee?

"Will just hiring a bunch of senior executives in fancy roles solve the problems of transformation," Satvik asked Ajesh.

"It may not solve the revenue problem in the short term, but it shows the intent that Marshal has. It shows his long term view of the organization," Ajesh responded.

"I don't think so. It is a quick fix approach to divert attention from the deeper problems. Since Marshal has little clue on how to resolve a situation, it is an easy escape by hiring a bunch of people and presuming that the problems would vanish some way," Satvik replied.

"The transformation has to be kick-started at the CxO level and slowly it can seep into next level," said Ajesh.

"To tell you honestly, Marshal's actions are creating more friction in our organization. The senior executives are increasingly getting disconnected with the next management layer like us. They believe that we are responsible for all the historical mistakes and we resist anything that changes the status quo," Satvik replied.

"But we are to be blamed for this equally. We believe that since the senior management is new, they must be wrong always. They bring much needed fresh ideas and need our support for executing the ideas," said Ajesh.

"They have no clue how the organization works, have little intent to learn and have no regard for the existing culture. They simply force their decisions top down. Instead of working together in a synchronized way, they are here to blame us as the potential weak link," Satvik added.

Marshal himself was increasingly coming under pressure that he had created with the new 10 billion dollar revenue target. His intentions were good – to set an aspirational goal to energize the employees. However, he realized that it was not having the desired impact. Most of the employees thought that the lofty targets were just to buy longer time for his transformation agenda; the higher the target, the longer the time horizon. Marshal realized that the second year would not be as kind to him unless something more fundamental was changed. He had to quickly identify the roadblocks and clear them before the execution of his plan.

Marshal had two options – take a pause, look at what was working and what was not and revise his approach, or continue with his current approach with increased conviction. It was like when one was driving to a destination under time pressure, he had to sometimes decide between increasing the speed of the car or slowing it down to find out shorter path and take a turn. The choice was between pressing the accelerator harder or pressing the brakes, pausing and re-strategizing.

Marshal was also aware that he was watched by all stakeholders now and his actions were scrutinized more minutely. Now the question for him was not only the organization's survival, but his own survival in the organization as well.

Since slowing down was not an option, Marshal became even more aggressive in implementing his policies. He would never want to hear 'no' for any initiatives that he would push. His management team was getting more scared to raise even genuine concerns in implementing his directives. This had an even worse outcome – Marshal only worked with a core team of executives who always agreed with his point of view. Creative Tech, which always encouraged open discussion was slowly becoming personality centric where decisions were made to please people rather than using sound management principles.

Marshal thought of an idea to speed up the transformation he was thinking of – the management consultants. He recalled Jonson Consulting were good at it. They came very handy, as he recalled from his previous organization's experience. Marshal called up John, his acquaintance with whom he had grown friendly during their last engagement. He liked their detailed data backed report to justify their findings.

"John – I want to speed up the digital transformation in my organization. I think the speed is way too slow. There are roadblocks that we need to clear," Marshal briefed John in the first meeting.

He added further, "Having spent more than a year now, I know what the problems are and how they can be solved. I just don't have enough data to back them up for some skeptics within and outside of Creative Tech."

John was used to such briefings before the start of his assignment. Management consulting assignments according to him was always a delicate exercise where sometimes the CEOs would engage the external consultants to add legitimacy to what they were planning already. It helped the CEOs to drive the change through the organization, especially the recalcitrant middle management. Marshal also needed the report to socialize with the board members, some of whom had started asking questions about the goal setting and approach to achieve the goals.

Jonson Consulting sent two senior consultants to the Bengaluru office of Creative Tech. John himself had travelled to India for this important assignment, another of his colleagues joined him from the local office. They moved around in the building, observing Creative Tech engineers and having short meetings to collect relevant data. Employees were suspicious of these consultants as if they were secret agents sent by Marshal.

Satvik wondered why the management consultants were so mistrusted, possibly due to the nature of the usual recommendations they make. He had told his team members as well to alert him as soon as any of the consultants approached them for any data or discussion.

John set up a meeting with all the project managers in the office. The meeting invite was sent from Marshal's office. Marshal also got an email sent to every manager.

From: Marshal Scott
To : All Managers and above

Sub: Engagement with Jonson Consulting

Dear Colleagues,

I am happy to share that we have engaged Jonson Consulting to help us accelerate faster in the digital transformation process. They have worked with best-in-class organizations in the past and helped them identify areas of improvements. They will conduct a six-week diagnostics, and benchmark that with similar companies.

I request you all to extend all possible support to John and his team.

Cheers,
M

An e-mail like above meant that any resistance to John and his team would be taken up seriously by Marshal.

"How will you identify the problem area in the company?" Satvik asked John.

"We have a diagnostic tool where if we feed Creative Tech data, it can tell you the area of improvement," John replied.

That looked like a magic wand, Satvik thought. While the whole organization was struggling to come to terms, a tool seemed too simplistic a solution.

"How does that tool work?"

"It has benchmark data of the best in class companies on key metrics; once we feed in Creative Tech data, we will know the red spots that need attention," John replied proudly.

"Can you share the benchmark with us beforehand?" Satvik requested them.

"No sir, the benchmarks are our proprietary information. It is our collective intelligence of many years of work across several organizations. In fact, when we collect the data, we make a promise to the client that it would never be shared with any other client in any form. Just like we will collect the data from you, but would never share with any other competing organization. We sign a non-disclosure agreement to protect the sanctity of each client," John was quite smart to handle naysayers like Satvik.

This essentially meant that Satvik and his team would have to agree with any recommendation that John would give, as their benchmark data could never be challenged.

Jonson Consulting did a comprehensive data gathering. They collected information like the number of running projects, average team size, number of defects, project overruns, etc.

They interviewed all the important stakeholders of Creative Tech. Though their presence was not welcome at the middle management level, the managers had no choice but to co-operate with them. Many believed such a problem solving exercise by an external consultant was futile , especially when the context was digital disruption which had little parallel in the past.

Anyway, the study was successfully completed and Jonson Consulting presented a comprehensive two hundred-page report to the Creative Tech Board. Satvik also got a copy of the summary note:-

> 'Our best in class benchmark suggests that average project team size in Creative Tech is 40% higher than the best in class companies. Productivity measured in revenue per employee is significantly lesser by 50%, going by the leading software companies' data. Our analysis suggests that that the current workforce in Creative Tech can be optimized by 30%.'

The report also endorsed the broad contours of Marshal's long term goals. It mentioned that there were certain critical success factors to achieve the goal, some of them being – more focus on the innovation team set up in the US and de-focus from the routine transactional work. As per the report, there was a need to change the workforce composition to make it more global from the current Indian set up. This meant that more people needed to be hired at the US centres.

'Your middle management is broken' was another conclusion of the consulting report. Satvik thought it was amusing that the troubled organizations pay fat sums to the consultants to tell them that poor middle management was the culprit in strategy execution that was defined by the senior management. So, every time the CEO of the organization hires a management consultant to fix their problem – one team that fears the most is middle management – they end up being laboratory rats.

Marshal felt vindicated with the report. He presented that to the board to reassure them that even the reputed management firm agreed with his approach with some minor alterations. The board backed Marshal with even greater conviction. Marshal suddenly felt the burst of energy that he badly needed at this critical juncture.

Satvik believed that with the Jonson Consulting assignment getting over, the employees could breathe easy. However, this started a slew of HR initiatives that were aimed at optimizing costs. Satvik found it amusing because these were exactly the things Marshal had opposed when he had joined Creative Tech. Now in the garb of Jonson Consulting, was he reversing his own point of view, Satvik wondered.

Though Marshal was more determined about his direction, the team at the ground level was getting more restive. Satvik had difficulty in explaining to his programmers on various issues including changing HR policies, slowing promotions and growth prospects. Some of the team members believed that there was differential treatment between the innovation team hired in the US and the existing technical team in India. Even the allocation of the type of work was problematic.

Few years back, the HR department used to collect periodic data to understand the pulse of the team and a situation like this would have easily got red flagged for corrective actions. Once, Satvik complained about the laxity in HR process to manage team motivation.

"But, we have such a low attrition rate, we have far lesser than the last year. Our policies must be one of the better ones," the HR anchor responded proudly.

In the past, an unhappy employee easily found another job and left the organization; this helped keep the overall environment in Creative Tech positive. If there is a large number of disgruntled employees and they remain in the system for a longer period of time, they make the work environment even more toxic.

Satvik realized that the hiring game was changing in favour of the employers. In the past, when the IT industry was booming and every company was looking for skilled resources, the employees were calling the shots. Some of them would have three or four offers in the waiting from the rival organizations. The success criteria for the HR was to have high employee retention and large-scale recruitment. It used to keep them on their toes.

Of late, the jobs in the market had come down. Almost all the companies were in the digital disruption journey and had pretty much stopped hiring. The employee scene was turning so bad that for the first time, some people were actively talking about setting an employee union to stop the exploitation by large IT companies. Just few years back, even a thought like that would have been laughable.

Another unintended outcome of the consulting assignment was that Marshal started several strategic projects with cryptic names.

Marshal had a unique liking for acronyms. Since he had joined as CEO, he had come up with several projects that would have esoteric names like NASA projects. Satvik was intrigued in the beginning to hear those fancy names. A name like 'Project Galileo' was deliberate to inspire some awe and fancy.

Many a times, they were a kind of rebranding of some of the existing running programs. For example, there was already a program to create an intelligent analytical platform that was domain agnostic. Marshal created a new project named 'BITS' which could be the new age AI solution – an intelligent robot with expert insights. Marshal was very bullish about BITS – it was his brainchild, his own idea. He created a high profile team of the best resources and gave them a task to conceptualize and create the future of Creative Tech in program BITS. This was his answer to digital disruption.

Marshal called for an analyst briefing and he introduced BITS as an answer to all questions that the clients of Creative Tech had been asking. Some of the media houses were really impressed with the bold vision.

'Creative Tech finally sows the seeds of innovation in BITS,' reported one newspaper next day.

'Creative Tech dares to dream with BITS' – headlined another business daily.

"BITS is the physical manifestation of the digital dream of Creative Tech. It is a platform powered by new age digital technologies, e.g. AI, Blockchain, IOT, cloud and big data. It is domain agnostic, it can be used to solve many problems in today's world, be it the field of banking, healthcare, telecom, aviation or any other. Our initial pilot of the platform had been hugely encouraging and some of our large clients have started deploying it already," Marshal described BITS in more detail.

It seemed as if BITS was created for the innovation hungry media. Marshal somehow was happy with this sudden change in focus – it seemed to have solved one problem for him. Earlier he had struggled to articulate the new vision for Creative Tech. BITS seemed to have solved that problem. The acronym could potentially encompass all future ideas. The only problem was the execution – because no one else in the executive team knew what it meant, leave aside how to create it.

As time passed, Marshal's faith in BITS increased even further. For Satvik, it was still an enigma. He genuinely tried to understand the grand plan behind BITS a few times, but to no avail. Slowly his clients started asking about it and Satvik just tried to avoid the discussion so as not to embarrass himself with the lack of awareness on a key initiative of Creative Tech.

Marshal explained this confusion as the real beginning of the transition that they all must eventually succeed in. No transition ever is without any pain. Cannibalization of business is a practical strategy when it comes to moving to the new business model. The digital transformation was never going to be easy anyway.

Satvik's understanding of the BITS development was slightly different. In this long legacy based company, Marshal was eagerly looking to call something of his own – an idea that germinated with him, a project that no one else could tell him stories about because it was his brainchild. In a way, he was looking for his own Creative Tech in this company. BITS was his reflection and for the first time Marshal felt part of this company.

"Everyone is talking about BITS but no one has a clear idea of how it is going to be implemented. Isn't it a recipe for disaster and disappointments?" Satvik asked Ajesh.

"There are two ways to drive innovation – bottom up and top down. If the company has a long legacy and transition is difficult, it is advisable to drive it top down. Marshal is trying to articulate the vision and forcing the next level to innovate," Ajesh tried to explain the rationale behind Marshal's action, which was not very evident.

"Isn't it the same like Marshal gave a top down revenue target of 10 billion, hoping it will somehow happen? We are already one year into it and don't see any sign of that happening," Satvik was less optimistic of this top down innovation approach.

Marshal realized that a new product like BITS may not find an easy acceptance in the organization. In order to push this, he created a new sales incentive plan for people who could sell BITS more than the traditional business. Under normal circumstances, the sales people would have jumped at an opportunity like this, but in this case, the sales team was clueless. They still tried and in some cases landed up with half-baked solutions and dissatisfied customers. Incidentally, all these failures were attributed to the lack of execution capabilities within the team. For Marshal, BITS strategy could possibly have no holes. Anyone questioning the objective was naturally relegated to the old school of thought.

For most of the employees, there was a clear directive to deploy BITS in the existing program.

"We need to deploy BITS in all the 45 banks that our team is engaged with," Robert directed Satvik as an order from Marshal.

"How can we force any platform to our own clients? We need to have a clear value proposition for them and hope that they buy," Satvik replied.

"At this point, we are not worried about the revenue. We just need to deploy the platform in as many client programs as possible. Our idea is to gather data, the platform will learn from the data and at some point it will start the delivering the real value. That will be the real opportunity to monetize BITS," Robert told Satvik.

"Does this mean that we sell BITS for free to our existing clients?" Satvik tried to simplify the convoluted argument.

"Let it be free in the beginning," Robert said.

Satvik soon realized that Marshal was using a clear strategy to report higher earnings from his new platform. Once BITS was deployed in the current program, that project was earmarked as BITS driven digital business account. This was akin to window dressing while reporting the digital revenue.

BITS was also a new answer to the now increasingly skeptic Creative Tech Board. In the past, the board had grilled Marshal on what immediate steps he was taking to transform the company. Marshal prepared an elaborate presentation full of all futuristic technology. Most of the board members looked at the presentation with awe. Eventually they agreed that Marshal was taking the company on the right track. The chairman said that this time Marshal had not only shared his idea, but shaped it well for execution.

CEO's Act 2

This was the 10th quarterly result for Creative Tech that Marshal was presenting. He had completed a little over two years, with his plan of turnaround of the company. Though the quarterly results used to be a great occasion to highlight the vision of the company, Marshal realized that he was increasingly being bogged down by the past numbers. This quarterly result was not good. For the first time, the company had missed its own revenue forecast and profitability tumbled. He was more worried about the grilling by the media. The share price was down more than 7% on the date of the result announcement.

"Marshal – what do you think of your target of 10 billion USD in five years? We are halfway through the period and looks like the company has still not taken off," one of the reporters asked Marshal.

Marshal had prepared a defence for the bad performance of the last quarter. He had also replaced three business heads of the badly performing units. Though he had the list of other corrective actions that he took, he was not quite prepared for the five year target question.

"We are still at it," Marshal replied.

He added further, "Any transformation is resource hungry for the first two years, after which it starts showing benefits. We have started well on the excellent execution of our strategy and we will catch up with the lost time. We are also evaluating some of the great acquisitions that will help us in achieving our long term goals."

There were many questions that were increasingly getting difficult for Marshal. He realized that at times he was getting incoherent and contradicted himself. The media was getting critical of each and everything that was not even related to the company performance. One of them asked if he had failed to culturally assimilate into the same organization that he inherited. Some asked if his stay in US was the reason for disenchantment of many of India based employees. He was also critically questioned for hiring expensive resources and encouraging avoidable expenses. The same actions, for which the media had earlier hailed him, were being discussed as the reasons for the failure. The media can be nasty and Marshal was realizing at this difficult time, they happily attacked their hero when he was found faltering. They just needed interesting stories for their audience.

Marshal already had several internal challenges. Now he had another one added to it – damaging media reports. Every now and then, a mainstream publication would write something about Creative Tech and how Marshal was grappling with the situation. They would give reference to some unknown sources and publish gossip about the company. Some of it was partly true as well, but Marshal wondered how the information reached the media. He suspected there were some people in his own leadership team who wanted him to fail. He issued strict advisory for everyone not to share anything with outside news agencies. The bad press continued however, and got only nastier with time.

The Creative Tech board was also asking Marshal questions – whether he would be able to meet the target that he set himself? What were his plans to speed up the growth in the next few quarters?

Now Marshal was realizing that he may have set a target way too high without much groundwork. His management team had always warned him, but Marshal could never accept their view. After all, he could never go to board and present a moderate target while proposing his transformation program. The board hired a high flying expensive CEO not to have an average industry growth. So even though his management team did not agree, Marshal did not have a choice but to present a goal like 10 billion USD revenue in five years, although he had no idea how to get there. Marshal took a brave step that time and a risk that he would get there somehow by driving his team hard.

So when the board grilled him hard that the current rate of growth was not sufficient to meet the target, Marshal pushed forward his other golden idea – 'acquisition'. Marshal proposed that he was betting big on acquiring a new-age company that would help multiply the revenue numbers. Some of the FinTechs in Silicon Valley were identified as the potential targets. Marshal convinced everyone that this also presented an opportunity for the company to reinvent in the new technology area. It would help to adopt the culture of new-age companies. Marshal had few companies shortlisted in the area of Automation and AI. Marshal thought it was better to bet on them to grow big rather than Creative Tech showing any sign of meteoric rise.

Few weeks later, Satvik received a letter from Marshal which was addressed to all the employees.

From: Marshal Scott
To: All employees of Creative Tech

Dear Friends,

It gives me immense pleasure to announce addition of a new product in our portfolio. We have in-principle agreement to acquire a new company called AutomateIT. The company is based in Silicon Valley and has some very innovative offerings that can be used for our clients across different geographies. As we continue our journey in the digital transformation, this acquisition will help us accelerate further.

We will continue to look for more acquisitions in the coming months.

Best regards,

M

Satvik looked at the website of the company. It was a three-year old startup of less than a hundred people. Their tools claimed to use new-age technologies like machine learning and neural network to provide predictive system support and maintenance. They were also actively looking at opportunities for funding. There were several startups like that in the Silicon Valley. Some of them would also grow into unicorns.

"I am not against the acquisition of new-age startups," Satvik was discussing with Ajesh, "but can they be the answer to the revenue growth of our company?"

Ajesh replied, "Some of them do have the potential to become the Facebook or the Google of tomorrow."

"Can one really bet on finding another Facebook or Google in the current Silicon Valley? And if there was really one, why would they easily look for being an acquisition target. Though I admire the entrepreneurial culture in Silicon Valley, some of the startups lack vision. They only look for an early exit to make some quick cash," replied Satvik.

For Marshal, acquisition was a perfect tool to drive change, both technologically and culturally. He was not bothered about the cultural clash, rather he thought it was better in a way to adopt new things. More than anything else, it gave him little more of the breathing space and time. There were some reports that the AutomateIT acquisition was overvalued, but Marshal brushed them aside as another hit job from media. He was of the opinion that for high value purchase, one had to shell out handsome money. That's how it worked in the valley.

Marshal was very articulate about the value that AutomateIT brought to Creative Tech. He sent individual mails to key business leaders and sales representatives that he would personally track the client adoption of this tool. He also announced special incentives for those who would be able to sell and deploy these tools. He took it upon himself to make this acquisition a grand success, something that would help him go for more.

When Satvik spoke to his colleagues, most of them did not understand the value that this tool brought and how to propose this to the clients. No one asked Marshal this question directly though, in fear of risking his anger. How can an employee be so ignorant about something that the CEO has been talking about since some time? Marshal gave target to everyone on selling AutomateIT. Suddenly the whole organization looked like becoming an aggressive sales arm of a newly acquired tool that was struggling as a startup to find new clients.

Next month, there was another mail from Marshal.

From: Marshal Scott
To: Satvik Saxena

Subject: Reduction in headcount

Satvik,

*We are getting very encouraging results about the market
success of our new acquisition, AutomateIT. One of the great
benefits of this has been that many of the client teams have been
able to reduce their headcount by up to 40%. I look forward to
your plans on reducing the current staffing numbers by at least
30%.*

*We will reskill these employees in upcoming technologies
and deploy them in innovative work.*

Regards,
M

Satvik was already worried about how to meet his target to deploy
this newly-acquired tool that was becoming more of a menace. The
staff reduction was double whammy. Sometimes Satvik wondered if
Marshal even understood how his team worked on the ground. Satvik
suspected that all this was an excuse to cut cost in India as some of
the recent hires in the US were dragging the profitability low. Another
challenge was to explain it to the team and get the work done with
30% lesser resources.

Next week, there was a mail from the HR department that the
salary increments and promotions have been frozen till further notice.
Satvik himself had hardly seen any increments for last couple of years.
At least his junior team members looked at it as some motivation. All
these austerity measures hit the middle management the most. The
senior management team would somehow manage their own salary

raise by getting some board approvals. Even when the employees' salaries were stagnant, the executive management saw meteoric rise in theirs. If some people raised questions about executive compensation, they were quickly shown how corporate America pays their executives well.

Creative Tech was set up on the unsaid principle of 'earn in dollars and spend in rupees'. Most of the employees were based in India while the clients were mostly in the US and Europe. This provided the company with perfect opportunity and it grew rapidly. The company had a healthy profit margin for many years. The hiring in US, however, changed that model quickly. It also added expenses in dollars. This was another worry for Marshal, as the profit margins were increasingly coming under pressure.

"The outsourcing industry is set up for a massive reversal. Marshal is doing the right things for Creative Tech," Ajesh said.

May be he was right. Reading various expert analysis, it was clear that this was the new era of insourcing; outsourcing was coming under intense scrutiny from all quarters.

Amongst all these challenges, Satvik was missing the honest conversations that he used to have with Vikas. Satvik had almost forgotten about him in the last few months. He felt an urge to connect with him.

"Hello Vikas, hope you are doing fine; it has been a while and I thought it would be great to catch up," Satvik called up Vikas.

"Sure, let us meet over a cup of coffee this Sunday evening," Vikas was more than receptive in responding.

Opportunities after Corporate Life

It had been about a couple of years since Vikas had left Creative Tech. Satvik had not tried to connect with him after he had left, partly because of his own hectic work schedule and partly because he was not sure how Vikas would react to his own association with his erstwhile company. It was never easy to deal with a sudden job loss in a country like India, with social stigma attached with it as well. Still, Satvik was curious to know how Vikas was coping with the situation. Satvik also wanted some advice on how to deal with his own situation in the light of increasing challenges.

When Satvik met Vikas, he found him in good health and spirits. Satvik was happy to see that Vikas had not only overcome the disappointment of his job loss, he was able to discuss the topic eloquently. On the contrary, Satvik looked more stressed because of his work situation.

"How have you been spending the last two years?" Satvik asked Vikas.

"Well, when I moved out of Creative Tech, I did not know what to do. Just few months back, my wife had taken a break from her job as she was finding it difficult to manage our young kids. I did not object to it, as I was never constrained financially. I could not immediately gather enough courage to tell her the truth.

"I told her that I have to go outstation for a month on some company work. I just hoped she did not get to know about it from others.

"Few times in your life, you have to press the 'restart' button. It was that moment for me. I had to reconstruct myself all over again, from zero and rebuild brick-by-brick. It was like I was driving at a high speed in my car towards my destination, hopefully to become the CEO of Creative Tech one day, when I hit the wall with a bang. My car broke into pieces and my journey came to an end even before I realized it.

"I was not in the best condition to apply for another job. I decided to take a break and indulge in an activity that I always wanted to do but could not because of my hectic work schedule.

"I went for a fifteen-day trek in the Himalayas as part of an adventure camp with unknown people. In hindsight, it was probably one of my best decisions. For fifteen days, we were living in a pure natural set up at 10,000 feet, the area mostly covered with snow. It was not only an escape from lingering worries, but was also rejuvenating.

"You know, I have a fear of heights. Few times, I felt sick, but the hilly terrain eventually helped me overcome that. During some of the adventure sports like rock climbing and river crossing, I realized my own fears and I overcame them. We had to trek the whole day, then cook our food and finally pitch our tents to sleep in. I had the soundest sleep that I had had in the last many years. Also, since I did not have my phones, TV or social media, I had a lot of time to think and reflect in that setting. For the first time, I realized I had taken a break from the mindless running and was experiencing something more profound.

"As part of the daily rituals, we were expected to meditate for an hour. I reflected on the incidents of the last few years and I was getting more insights into my own actions and behaviour. Nature is a great teacher, if you carefully observe her. It can lift your spirits when you are down. In those jungles and mountains, there are millions of creations and destructions happening at the same time. If you look in isolation, each destruction is a crisis, but they are all part of a cycle that perpetuates itself. Trees dry up, animals die, but the jungle continues to live in the harmony for thousands of years. I saw my crisis as an opportunity, a larger part of a creative destruction process," Vikas went on for some time.

"What were the key revelations that you had?" Satvik asked Vikas.

"First and foremost, I realized the mistakes that I was making. I had stopped learning new things. In the last five years or so, I hardly learned anything new. I recall when I had joined Creative Tech, I was full of curiosity. I used to spend personal time to learn new technology and programming languages. You must have heard about the car game that I had created during the first year of my joining. It was fun, but also helped me to learn new things. Slowly, with time, I started depending only on the previous learning rather than understanding new things. My learning stopped and I started managing people and things. I got more involved in stakeholder management, but my own personal growth stopped. I used to hear about disruptive technology and new things, but never got enough motivation to drive myself to learn. Instead of learning new things, I developed a skeptical approach for upcoming changes. It was so unlike me," Vikas responded.

"Do you mean to say that you find yourself responsible for your layoff?" Satvik could not agree with this conclusion.

"Absolutely – once you get over the initial anger and feeling of being a victim, you realize that most of such incidents are triggered by the individuals themselves. Many individuals refuse to see the change and change themselves," Vikas responded.

"Aren't Marshal's policies responsible for this chaos as well?" Satvik was not convinced with the argument put forward by Vikas. He thought Vikas was being too idealistic and justifying things by being too gracious.

"I spent less time analyzing what Marshal was doing and more time on what I could have done. I realized what happened to me was more to do with my own failure to correct myself," Vikas said.

"That does not mean that what Marshal is doing is perfectly fine, just that I have little control over it. I tried to understand the impact of his changes. My analysis says he is as clueless as many of us. He is right in talking about the forthcoming disruptions, but does not quite know the right response. He is trying to navigate a boat in the rough sea, but he does not quite know how long the storm will last. But as leader, he has to act," Vikas added further.

Satvik was enjoying the conversation with Vikas.

"Okay, let us go for a smoke," Satvik recalled his insightful suggestions during the smoking breaks.

"I have stopped smoking," Vikas said.

Satvik could not believe that. Vikas had been a chain smoker. This was one thing that Vikas had said he could never do, whatever be the reward.

"Yes Satvik, during my visit to the mountains, I was not allowed to carry cigarettes. For the few days I thought about it constantly – later I forgot. I was happy to know that I could live without cigarettes. Later I thought, if I could live without them for fifteen days, I could also live without them forever," Vikas said.

"And you quit smoking?" Satvik said in disbelief.

"See, Satvik, many a times we do not recognize our own will power and potential. We just blame everyone except ourselves. Even for the smoking, I blamed the continued work pressure while it was me who needed to take appropriate action," Vikas replied like a sage.

"It is really nice talking to you, Vikas. It seems the meditations and reflections have really helped you. How do you explain the behaviour of Marshal?" Though Vikas had moved on, Satvik was still stuck at what was happening in Creative Tech.

To explain the situation at Creative Tech, Vikas told Satvik a story.

"Once a struggling CEO of a company was replaced due to perceived failure to manage company challenges. The new CEO, before taking charge, asked the previous one what were the lessons he learnt and what were his suggestions to manage the difficult situation in the company. The outgoing CEO said that he would not be able to explain that. However, to help him, he had left three chits in the office drawer. The chit had the lessons and suggestions on what to do. Each chit needed to be opened one-by-one after each year of his leadership.

"The new CEO opened the chit marked as 'Year 1'. The chit said 'Buy Time – blame the company's current practices, culture and people for their current state'. He did the same and one year passed by. The problems did not look any better though.

"Next year he opened the second chit marked as 'Year 2'. The chit read – 'Carry out rampant reorganization'. The new CEO followed the same, and even swapped the roles of HR and business heads. He reappointed the sales head as head of finance. He also hired several new faces in key senior roles to manage the change.

"The problems however did not disappear. They only became more aggravated with time. Finally, during the third

*year he opened the 3ʳᵈ chit that was lying there. He got a shock
to read what was written on that 'Time to write down your
own three chits'."*

This story captured the current state of some professional CEOs who
were brought in to steer a turnaround that they had little idea about.
Their own commitment to the turnaround stories was questionable.
There have been successful turnarounds and charismatic CEOs, no
doubt, but going by what Marshal had been doing so far, he'd possibly
fit right into the story.

"So does it mean that Marshal will leave Creative Tech after three
years?" Satvik asked Vikas.

"I hope he does not leave and logically completes the
transformation that he has started. But I would not be surprised if
he does. If he is really a visionary leader, he would carry through his
promises by executing it rather than creating new promises," Vikas
was quite direct in saying that.

"This looks too simplistic. Doesn't the board know the tricks that
CEOs play for their own survival? Aren't they smart enough?" Satvik
asked further.

"How would the board act differently even if they knew the tricks
that CEOs play? They have to respond to the shareholders that they
have taken the right action by changing the CEO and hiring the most
deserving one," Vikas responded.

Satvik realized that even if not entirely, part of what Vikas was
saying made sense. Satvik was thinking that Vikas would be angry
and bitter due to his layoff. On the contrary, he was offering words
of wisdom that were useful to him. Sometimes the unintended
consequence of a seemingly bad incident could be good as well.

Satvik was also impressed with the way Vikas had handled
himself post his layoff. It is not the event but our response to the same

that makes the difference between success and failure. Satvik was confident that Vikas would probably be able to convert his misery to an advantage for him.

"The other big learning that I had was about my own insecurities. I remember someone telling me a joke – there are three poisons in this world; first one is salary and rest two do not matter," Vikas said.

"We are all dependent on our salary for our financial needs, aren't we? In a way, many of us do work for a salary," Satvik responded.

"My reading of various books and experience in the corporate world suggest that the salary mindset is the biggest obstacle for our creativity and learning today." Vikas seemed sure about it.

Satvik did see some logic in what Vikas was saying. The salary phenomenon probably was more of an outcome of the industrial revolution where a large number of people were required to do repetitive jobs and hence their remuneration could be fixed based on the outcome that they produced. The era of mass production was perfectly suited for salary society. The current disruption in digital technology was making some of these jobs automated. The fixed salary for repeating a set of predefined skills would be surely under threat. More creative people could definitely find a job, but they would not be in the same 'salary mindset'.

"Another important lesson that I learnt was that we put too much emphasis on the organized secure job and underestimate our own ability to find gainful employment. For the first few months, I was on my own, but soon found out that there are various ways to do something interesting and at the same time support myself financially. When I meet some entrepreneurs here, they have many stories to tell. They tried many things, failed at some but improved at the next attempt. They had been undergoing continuous learning in that way. Most importantly, they tried out all that they wanted to do in life.

"The ultimate professional success is when you do what you love to do and eventually get paid for that. That is happiness in the true sense. When you have your own story and you are not a character in someone else's story. It is not that entrepreneurs don't work as hard. Probably they end up working 100 hours a week just to avoid working 50 hours for an employer. It is just that their work is no longer work; it is more of play," Vikas said.

Satvik agreed with Vikas that the entrepreneurs had eventful journeys – of successes and failures, while most of the employees of Creative Tech had no stories other than saying they worked for the company all their lives. They never bothered to experiment with their deeper interests and passions as they were always constrained by what was expected by the organization. It had made them dumb followers – grudging order takers who always complained about everything. They were losing their creativity every day.

CEO's Act 3

It was appraisal time – a yearly ritual that had become more of a balancing act of late. This time the unusual directive from the HR was to mandatorily put 20% of the current team members as under performers.

Most of the managers were already struggling with the increased attrition and dwindling motivation of the team members. This could be devastating, Satvik thought.

"If we believe that we have a sound hiring process and decent training process, how can 20% of our team members become underperformers all of a sudden?" Satvik asked his HR anchor.

"It is to inculcate the high performance culture in the organization," the HR anchor was already prepared with the answer.

"A high performance culture can be inculcated by giving more rewards to the deserving employees. A mandatory 20% bottom performer identification will only create a sense of panic among the employees; it will add to the negativity," Satvik continued.

Satvik soon realized that there was no point in discussing this with the HR as they were merely order takers. It was surprising how

Creative Tech, which was known for its caring employee policies, had digressed to this state where it was seen as so unfriendly.

The appraisal exercise was more of a damage minimization exercise for the team. After all the optimization, Satvik was left with a team of seventy people, so he needed to identify at least fourteen people who needed to be marked as underperformers. There were many other HR guidelines to make it look a fair exercise, e.g. people on sabbatical or long leave couldn't be marked as underperformers. Woman friendly policies ensured that those on maternity leave could not be singled out, even if they were bad performers. In the past, there was no mandatory earmarking like this. The bell curve was eliminated as per new policies from Marshal. But these were even more draconian.

The difficult part of these appraisals was that almost all the identified underperformers would eventually dispute these ratings as per HR policy. So Satvik was sure that there would be at least fourteen disputes on his evaluations where Satvik would have to defend why he rated the employee so low. The review committee at times reversed these ratings and the managers got the warning letter instead. Some of these rating review discussions used to be very difficult to conclude.

"Do you really believe that such a policy will create high performance work culture?" Satvik asked Ajesh who used to have an opinion on such things always.

"I see it more as a cost cutting measure," Ajesh responded.

"You will soon get a directive that the bottom performing employees would be asked to leave the organization," he added further.

"And Marshal will show this as reduction in employee cost, translating into higher per employee revenue and increased profit."

Satvik was not happy with such a deceptive game.

"This has been a common tool for American companies to reduce cost, and Marshal is using it now. Though it hits the company in the long term, in the short term, it shows increased performance and even better share prices. The increased shareholder value is the most important KPI for a CEO. This may even get him a further hike in his salary," Satvik told Ajesh.

The other forms of cost cutting also started showing in different areas. The office transport charges were increased, project party budget disappeared and even small discretionary employee expenses were curtailed. The promotions and salary hikes had been stopped a few quarters earlier already. Looking at these changes one could only conclude that the company was making a loss.

Another thing that Satvik was struggling with was the expectations of his junior team members. He found it so difficult to explain it to Raman, one of the brightest software engineers in his team.

"I have been waiting for my promotion for the last three years. I hope I get it in this appraisal cycle," Raman said.

"I hope you are aware of the organizational context. We are going through a difficult transformation currently. Though I am happy with your performance, I don't think that the promotion is likely," Satvik tried not to give him any false hope.

"It was the same thing that you told me the last cycle and assured me that this cycle it will surely happen," Raman replied.

Raman was the best performer in the team. Under normal circumstances, he would have got his promotion much earlier, but Satvik did believe some of these people refuse to understand the larger context. If there were no promotion slots at the organization level, there was very little that he could do. As a manager, Satvik was trained not to show helplessness or disconnect with the organizational directives, otherwise he would lose even the little respect that he had as a manager.

Satvik assured Raman to try his best to present the case for promotion. There was little doubt in his mind however that Raman would start looking out for another job soon. Satvik's problem was not only with Raman, there were expectations built up in everyone's mind based on past data. Satvik's team was slowly degenerating into collective under performance and there was hardly anything that he could do.

Satvik felt like walking up to Marshal and telling him that his transformation was breaking the backbone of the company. All the talk of digital transformation and AI would eventually fall flat if we don't have enough motivated people in the organization. Satvik used to hear earlier that the real asset of Creative Tech was its people. The stock value of Creative Tech became zero when all the employees left the office and zoomed back when they came back to the office next morning. The real asset on the balance sheet was its people.

On second thought, Satvik suspected that Marshal was doing this deliberately. It couldn't be that he was unaware of the impact. After all, he had scores of advisors and executives to support him. May be, he wanted to deliberately induce the pain in the system so that some people would leave. Probably he believed efficiency would increase automatically and once we had a lower headcount, the AI adoption would automatically increase. His intent could possibly be right, but Marshal was playing a dangerous game.

Anyway, Satvik's current problem was to handle disgruntled employees like Raman so that he did not spoil the overall team environment.

Raman left the organization after one month of his appraisal. Satvik was surprised how people at the junior level could still so easily switch jobs, and for a moment Satvik envied Raman. Satvik knew, even if he tried, he would not be able to find another job so easily. It was ironical that even though his experience had increased in the last many years, his employability had reduced. Satvik was getting more entangled in the work that he was doing, with no immediate escape.

While the employees in Creative Tech were under duress, Satvik read the following news in *The Business Times*:

> 'Creative Tech Board has decided to extend the tenure of Marshal, their CEO by another two years. The extension has been granted keeping in mind the digital transformation that is underway currently. Marshal's initiatives have started showing positive outcomes that is clearly evident from increased profitability and per person revenue.
>
> With this extension, the board has also agreed to increase Marshal's salary to seven million USD, part of which will be linked with the company performance and provided in the form of stock options.'

While Satvik thought Marshal was failing in his transformation agenda, the board thought it otherwise and rewarded him even further.

Satvik used to have a weekly catch-up call with Robert. It was a set up based on the insistence of Robert. Robert wanted to be abreast with what was happening in the Bengaluru office. It was a video conference late in the evening for Satvik, which used to be early morning time for Robert. Satvik had never met him personally, so this video call was the only personal interaction that Satvik used to have.

"I am happy to inform you that I have been promoted as the new vice president in Creative Tech," Robert told Satvik.

"Congratulations Robert, this is good news, but I am really surprised because our unit's revenues have still not risen. We are still off the target," Satvik responded.

"Our unit has been identified as the best in cutting the waste. We have optimized our team by 30%. I have also been able to set up the small innovation team here in the US office. These are no insignificant achievements," Robert responded.

"Excuse me, Robert, reducing the team size in India was an awful decision. Sooner or later we will have to bear the consequences," Satvik could not hold back his anger.

"Are there any more promotions in the executive ranks?" Satvik asked grudgingly.

"There are six more people who have got promoted to VP, three to Senior VP and two have been appointed as Executive VP," Robert said.

"So, it had been raining promotions at the VP level. We don't have promotion slots for the junior most engineers in our team and here we have so many promotions at the senior level? Isn't it complete disregard to sense and reason?" Satvik was angry at these revelations.

When he further learned the names of the people who had been promoted, he was in a bigger shock. Five out of these people had only joined Creative Tech in the last one year, and the remaining six had been selected from the long timer list. Marshal had just balanced it out so that no one blamed him for the favouritism. One thing was clearly evident though – all eleven of them worked very closely with Marshal.

"What amazes me is that none of the employees at the ground level would even be aware of the contribution of these newly promoted VPs," Satvik responded.

"Sat-vik, the VP promotions are not done by popularity contests from junior employees," replied Robert. He had a peculiar way to pronounce his name by adding a pause while saying Sat-vik.

Satvik didn't recall hearing anything else after this VP promotion news. He became numb.

It was not that Satvik was expecting a promotion himself. Not because he did not think he deserved it, but because he thought that the organization was going through a difficult time. But looking at these unexpected VP promotions, Satvik thought he had been fooled. The only senior person he could discuss this with was Rajendran.

"How did Robert get promoted? He never meets the clients, has not even met his team in India and has done nothing significant in the last twelve months," Satvik said to Rajendran.

"The strange thing is, I was not even consulted," Rajendran replied.

"I think Marshal has done it just to avoid attention on his own salary hike," Satvik told Rajendran.

"Secondly, these promotions clearly smack of nepotism and sycophancy. At least Robert was not deserving of any promotions."

"You need to raise an objection about Robert's promotion. You have access to the board. I can share all the data," Satvik replied.

"It wouldn't work. The whole show is managed by Marshal himself and I will be a lone dissenting voice."

"There must be some way to stop Marshal. Think about it, Rajendran. We need to act fast to safeguard the company."

"Marshal is not scared of anyone; the only thing I notice is that he is worried about media reports these days," Rajendran replied.

"Please do something. Now Robert will make my life miserable."

"Robert is a sideshow. The main protagonist of this saga is Marshal, and yes, we must do something about him," Rajendran hung up.

Satvik could not sleep that night. In the morning, he did not want to get up. Why should he go to office? He did not feel like walking up to the bus that day. But he thought about his team. After all, it was not their fault. There could be client escalations as well for such unplanned leaves, so he dragged himself. Satvik used to have a daily team meeting at 9 a.m. before starting the day. He had deliberately kept it at 9 a.m. so that everyone came on time.

"I heard there have been eleven VP level promotions in the company," Akhil told Satvik in the morning meeting. Akhil was the best technical lead in the team after Raman had left.

Satvik feigned ignorance, because he knew why that question was being asked.

But Akhil was clever. He had precise information. Raman, before he left, had warned him that it was foolish to expect any promotion in Creative Tech.

"What about Robert? I heard he has been made a VP. He must have shared the news with you, hasn't he?"

It was difficult to avoid this further.

"Yes, Robert has been made the VP. It is good news for our team as we will get more prominence."

"But it was only last month that you told us that the organization is not doing well and hence all the promotions have been frozen for the engineers. Even our bonus payments have been less than usual," Radhika added.

Satvik did not know how to respond. In reality, he agreed with Akhil and Radhika entirely. Satvik felt even angrier that such promotions were happening at the cost of him and his team. But here, in this meeting, Satvik was a management representative so he had to defend these promotions.

"For some of them, it was additional portfolio added with additional responsibilities."

"Either the company is doing well or it is doing badly – both can't be true at the same time. Also, it can't be true for junior employees and false for VPs!" Akhil banged the glass top that tilted on one side suddenly.

These were the unusual topics of discussion in the morning meeting. These meetings were supposed to be about the plan for the day, risk in the projects, etc. Of late these meetings seemed to include only such discussions. Satvik could not blame them. After all, what is there at the top of the mind always come out during project meetings.

"See Akhil, we can discuss that some other time, today we have to fix the five severe criticality defects," Satvik tried to avoid the topic when he did not seem to have any sound logic.

"Satvik, you can't dodge the question. When you give us work every day, we do that honestly. We go beyond the call of duty to finish the task. For the last three weeks, many of us have also worked during the weekends as we did not have enough people to complete the task. We feel cheated by these VP promotions," Akhil said.

"The extent of cost cutting in the organization is ludicrous. You know they have even stopped giving the few hundred rupees that they used to give for the project party," Radhika said.

"Not only that, even the toilet paper from the toilet is gone," one of Satvik's team members said.

Satvik did not want more data points on this. He very well knew that this cost cutting at every level was getting on everyone's nerves. To placate the team, Satvik used Ajesh's argument

"See, we can't do anything in such matter, let us focus on our work."

"It is wrong to say that we can't do anything," Akhil was getting more belligerent.

"What can we do? If we do not agree with certain management decisions, we can leave the organization. What else can we do?" Satvik said.

"Those who want to leave will anyway leave, that is an individual choice. Here we are talking of collective action," Akhil said.

"What do you mean?"

"We can all stop working for a few weeks or at least stop working any extra hours," Akhil said.

Akhil was speaking like a union leader in the production factories. Satvik recalled these discussions were common in his father's plant, but IT companies never had such things. There had never been the need. The HR of these organizations were hailed for having one of the most employee-friendly policies.

"See Akhil, these things do not work in IT companies. Threats of work slow and strikes happen only in the manufacturing companies mostly with unskilled labour. Here, if you try to act smart, they will fire you," Satvik offered a counter narrative.

"If we are alone, they will fire us, but if our entire team of seventy members goes on leave, they can't fire us. If they do, we will go to the media," Akhil said.

Satvik realized the discussion was going in an entirely different direction. Whether Akhil succeeded in creating an IT employee union or not was the question for another day. Satvik was more worried about the immediate client escalations.

Would Robert understand all these? He would simply say that Satvik had failed to manage the team. Satvik was already living with the threat of client escalations, now this was another dimension – threat of 'go-slow' from his own team members.

The Emerging Work
Culture of Startups

Satvik thought it was a good time to meet Vikas again and hear his perspective on the recent happenings in Creative Tech. Though Vikas was no longer with the company or Satvik's boss, his counsel always helped Satvik understand things better.

"Satvik, Marshal is probably right about a fundamental shift happening in this IT industry," Vikas said.

He added further, "If you recall earlier, there used be more focus on end-to-end IT projects. The banks would request for software solutions that would cater to all of their requirements including maintenance and support. They used to be large turnkey projects requiring a large number of people. All our processes were driven towards that scale and it worked very well. A large organization like Creative Tech was best suited to win these deals."

"Are those large deals not happening anymore?" Satvik was curious to know.

Vikas responded, "Based on what I have observed and you can also see, the large deals have got broken into several small sized deals. If earlier there was a deal of 10 million dollars that took on an average six months to win and five to six years to implement, the same has got broken into maybe twenty deals of less than 500k dollar size. This suddenly makes even a small firm with far lesser strength than Creative Tech, eligible to bid for the project. Here, the expected turnaround time has reduced from five to six years to months, and sometimes even weeks. These are deals that small agile companies are winning hands down. Creative Tech's processes are aligned mostly for large deals. We used to plan and hire engineers and scale them up."

Satvik asked again, "Is it happening due to increased adoption of the digital? What is digital, as I always find this word very confusing?"

Vikas replied, "It was happening since the last few years due to advancement in computing power and increased adoption of cloud. The real revolution was brought in by the mobile. For me, digital is mobility. A small device that used to be only for communication is a source of infinite computational power in the network."

Satvik agreed with Vikas, "When it comes to mobile app projects, our win-ability comes down. We take months to even prepare a proposal and deploy our engineers while the clients want the whole projects to be completed in a few weeks. In fact, now we have even stopped bidding for such projects because there is no point."

"Exactly – and this is the digital transformation that Creative Tech needs. Skill gap is just one part of the story. The entire organizational process needs to be recalibrated from large project to numerous small projects."

"I agree with you on that point. Strangely for this reason, we are facing competition from some of the very small firms and they are winning," Satvik added.

"I have been working with some of these startups of late. Now I can understand why a bank would be rather keen to engage these small companies than large players like Creative Tech. It is much more than technology reskilling – it is a cultural refresh. The sales team needs to learn how to sell small ticket items, the project delivery team needs to transform into a quick agile team and the organizational support processes like finance, HR need to be recalibrated to this new reality," Vikas was quite clear in his views.

"So, Marshal is partly right when he talks about creating urgency of the impending shift in the technology space? But I always find him repeating the same thing even to the extent of creating panic among team members. I find most of his meetings have become preaching sessions on how we are so off the target, but he himself has no immediate action point," Satvik said.

"Yes, Marshal is right in saying that. He is clearly defining what needs to be done. Where he flounders is how to get there. If you know your end destination, that is fine. But you must know your current position to clearly chart out a convincing plan of action. Marshal has little knowledge of current processes, challenges, skills and competencies. He has shown very little empathy to even understand them," Vikas shared his point of view.

"I think Marshal has contempt for the current processes. I recall how he once mocked at the current appraisal process, something that has been in place for so many years," Satvik added to Vikas.

"Marshal fails to connect with the same set of employees that he plans to transform. He tells them about an end dream, but refuses to engage on how to get there. In the process, he has got most of those employees turned against their own CEO. This has made his job even harder," Vikas said.

"Is that the reason star CEOs mostly fail in turning around corporations?" Satvik asked.

"A big change management of a large company like Creative Tech requires freshness and risk taking abilities of a bold CEO like a rank outsider, and employee empathy and appreciation like a long time insider. Both the traits, outsider and insider, are important in equal measure. To change a culture, you need to understand it first," Vikas responded.

"So, for what is corporate culture – a string of prevailing practices and stories? Is that something worth protecting when stakes are high, including its own survival?" Satvik asked.

Vikas responded, "I have never found a culture book in any organization. But each organization (large ones) has a distinct culture, though not codified ever. Culture is a series of folklore, stories and lessons that hold the organization together. It is the unseen glue that binds the stakeholders for a common vision for years together. It may not have a direct economic measure, but this is the only element that holds the organizations through several cycles of economic downturns and upsides. It is the un-codified collective learning of the organization and a future promise to reinvent itself based on those learnings."

Satvik was amazed at the clarity of thought that Vikas had on these issues of organizational change management. This discussion helped Satvik understand why Marshal was acting in the way he was. This conversation helped him see Marshal's perspective. Not everything that Marshal was doing could be called out as bad intent.

Vikas had started working with some of the startups in the city. His perspective had changed after seeing a different way of working. When Satvik insisted he visit his new workplace, Vikas was more than keen to take him there. It was a co-working area where different small companies shared space. It was a scene of disparate groups of people working on different ideas and engaged in passionate discussions. They did not have much infrastructure, nothing compared to the sprawling campus Creative Tech had.

Vikas said pointing at some of them, "This workspace may look very chaotic to you, but one thing I can vouch for is the energy and passion of these people towards their ideas. It is infectious when you see a bunch of young entrepreneurs believe that their idea has the potential to change the world and they work towards them. They may not have a lot of financial backing, but are willing to take risk and work hard."

Satvik realized Vikas was right. The place was full of positive energy and optimism. The same disruption that was worrying Satvik and his team in Creative Tech, was enthusing these people for creating something new. There was a perceptible difference in the motivation level of these people and Satvik's team members and colleagues. While Satvik's colleagues spent most of the time discussing the negative aspects of the transformation, the startups were positively engaged in working on the ideas of the future.

"Is it an end of large corporations as they would not be able to cope with the changing technological landscape?" Satvik asked Vikas.

"No, I don't think so. If you observe, there are many large companies like Amazon and Google that are growing even faster, to the extent of becoming large monopolies. These large companies are successfully able to create a federated set up where each entity behaves as a startup, with their own ideas and plans. They are able to provide institutional support to their different teams who work pretty independently with broader guidelines and objectives," Vikas said.

"This is where Creative Tech has failed probably. It is still a large nucleus where everyone looked up to the central command – be it new ideas, execution or leadership. Such large set ups are getting difficult to maneuver in the fast changing digital landscape," Satvik responded.

"Another very perceptible difference between the newly coming startups and Creative Tech is how the team members look at themselves as specialist vs generalist. In startups that I have seen, the folks are not bound by their job descriptions. There are no job descriptions to start with in the first place. People play different roles as the situation demands," Vikas said.

Satvik realized that large organizations were stuck in the employer-employee relations. The management team created ideas for execution by the employees. When the idea failed, the management blamed the employees for the failure, while the employees believed that it was a bad idea in the first place. On the contrary, the startups had progressed to collective ownership of ideas and their implementation. There was no division of labour there anymore.

Large organizations can be compared to communities that survive for centuries. Communities house a very balanced mix of those who are mature, run the present with their past knowledge vs those who are rebellious and challenge the established thoughts. A society needs sensible as well as what we call crazy challengers for its balanced prosperity and growth.

A part of the large organization should be allowed to be like rebel startups – a floating team of disruptive challengers and fearless dreamers.

"I agree with you that startups are going to be more successful in the new digital world, but still, why is it that we are not yet seeing thousands of startups coming into the mainstream? Why are there so few successful startups today and why do most of them fail?" Satvik asked Vikas.

Vikas responded, "Many startups today feel frustrated as to why their product is not a runaway success, in spite of solving the burning problem of the consumers. To explain this point, let me tell you a small story:

"In the 1990s, Dettol was the most dominant brand in the Indian market, a household name. However, it used to have

a pungent smell and caused a burning sensation. As a child, I recall feeling scared even at the mention of Dettol applied on a wound.

"Savlon got rid of these two problems when launched – it had a nice smell and no burning sensation. It had solved these two problems, and as per some lab reports, was a better germ killer than Dettol. Its tagline was 'healing without hurting'. It hoped to be a runaway success. The result was completely the opposite.

"The Savlon launch bombed. Dettol came up with a counter punchline: 'it hurts when it works' and the consumers believed Dettol.

"There are multiple lessons from the story on brand marketing and consumer behaviour. One that just the product being better is no success guarantee. The most important factor is the consumer trust that is built over a period of time. The consumers may complain, but they still trust a bank service rather than a one-year-old Fintech.

"Trust needs to be built over time. There's no overnight success even with the best solution."

Public Showdown

The town halls with the employees were getting increasingly problematic for Marshal. As employee discontent was growing, so was the expectation from the management to do something miraculous. Sometimes Marshal believed that these employees lived in their own world of entitlement – they clearly refused to see the disruption that was upon the whole company. Most of their questions were directed towards their personal benefits. Marshal thought this was a key difference between a true Silicon Valley company and a company like Creative Tech. Grudgingly, he had to face them as part of the routine employee interaction program.

This time, the auditorium was not even half filled to its capacity. It was in contrast with the first town hall when the auditorium was packed and people were sitting on the floor to listen to Marshal. The initial euphoria had given way to despondency and lack of trust in the management.

"Marshal, it has been more than two-and-half years that you have been the CEO of Creative Tech. After initial hikes in the first year, our annual compensation has been almost frozen. When we can see the salary hikes again?" was the first question from a very junior employee during the town hall.

Marshal always hated such questions. He thought instead people would ask questions about new inventions in technology, so he avoided any response to salary questions. He recalled how he once announced the 100% bonus payment for all the employees in the town hall during his initial days and all hell had broken loose. The finance department almost held him responsible for the loss in margin. It was a crisis that he had triggered by the sudden announcement. Marshal had learned his lessons. Moreover, freebies could not be given away every time employees wanted them.

Marshal had to control his anger to answer the question in a diplomatic way, "The compensation hike for the average employee is dependent on the company performance which depends on the overall industry. As we all are aware, the last few quarters have been particularly challenging for us, but with focus on our target, we will surely return to good growth."

There was another follow-up question. "There was a media report that Creative Tech has increased the salary of their management team significantly. There were significant hiring of high cost resources in Silicon Valley. How do you justify such action when the average employee in India does not get any hike?"

Marshal was used to such questioning from the media; he could still forgive them for their brashness. Marshal was aghast at the temerity of his own employees, raising doubts on his intentions in a public set up like this. In a smaller gathering, he would have got him fired. In a public meeting like this, however, the question needed a sober answer.

"We need to hire and retain high quality talent in the US, especially in Silicon Valley. They don't come cheap, and we need them to make a transition from low value work to high value work. For the executive compensation, we need to benchmark that from global standards and whenever there is a need, we continue to make corrections."

Most of the employees took the above statement as an assertion that Marshal would continue his strategy without caring for any criticism from his employees.

One of them asked further, "There have been rumours that the company is planning to lay off in India in order to hire employees in the costly locations in the US. To hire one person in US, four such people in India needs to be laid off. Is it fair for those employees who have spent years of service in the organization? Or are you just trying to create Creative Tech Americana?"

The question was full of accusation, mistrust, satire and sarcasm.

Marshal could not take this any longer.

"Such kind of questions have malicious intent. The management of Creative Tech takes appropriate decision as per business needs and those of you who really don't trust us are free to leave the town hall and even the company." Marshal wanted to send a stern message to the employees.

There was stunning silence after this statement from Marshal. A lot of employees got up and left the town hall midway. It was a very sudden and abrupt end to the Q&A session. Marshal also walked out of the town hall infuriated.

Marshal called Sujith, the HR head and asked,

"Do the employees expect me to answer individual salary and hiring policies in the town hall? Is that the organizational culture here?"

"Marshal, we don't restrict or advise the employees when they want to ask any question in the town hall. It has always been like that in Creative Tech."

"But not when some of the employees behave like idiots and ask questions like the media." Marshal was angry at the response.

"If you desire so, we will screen all the questions from now onwards before the town hall. However, I must insist that it has not been the culture at Creative Tech."

"Yes, I would like the questions and details of the employees asking such stupid questions in the town hall. And please don't always preach about your culture," Marshal almost shouted at Sujith.

Sujith was surprised to hear that even after two years, Marshal was considering himself an outsider while talking about the culture of Creative Tech. He had failed to assimilate as much as the employees had failed to transform to the new digital world.

The next day, there was a media storm. Someone had captured the video of the town hall and leaked it to some of the media houses. They were all publishing juicy stories for the showdown that Creative Tech had with their employees.

One headlines said – 'Creative Tech employee puts their CEO under notice.' Few others projected this outburst as an outcome of an attempt to Americanize what was essentially a poster child of the Indian IT technology. They all published stories using un-named sources, some of them even confidential information.

Marshal was amazed how the media had such deep links that they almost knew everything that was happening in Creative Tech, to the extent of sometimes even extrapolating and predicting what would happen next.

The media stories were taking up Marshal's significant time and energy. He tried to ignore them beyond a point, but it was not easy. Sometimes even the clients would ask him to comment on those stories. Each comment would give rise to more speculations and further erosion in credibility. Slowly even the other stakeholders like investors and shareholders started showing concern with negative media reports. The media was becoming a bigger disruptor than the technological disruption.

When Marshal had started his stint as the Creative Tech CEO, he was preparing himself for the digital trends and innovations that would be critical for the transformation of the organization. He had never imagined that three years down the line, he would spend the least amount of time on technology and most of his time and energy would be consumed in managing things like cultural changes, HR issues, stakeholder management and media handling. And the things were getting beyond control on various fronts. Some media reports were already calling him a failure at his work. He was slowly becoming a divisive figure within his own company as well.

The next Annual General Body of the company was a forgettable experience for Marshal. He looked somewhat vulnerable.

"I am amazed to see the cavalcade of fancy cars. I can't believe that you have even black commando bodyguards. I remember when Creative Tech management used to meet us like the common man during AGMs. Today you seem completely unapproachable," one old shareholder said during the Q&A session.

Some shareholders almost held Marshal guilty of taking the iconic organization down the path of destruction. Very few gave some concession to him, saying the entire industry was undergoing the transformation, hence it was not fair to single out only Creative Tech. Though Marshal was a person who always had clarity of thoughts in difficult situations, here he was pretty much frozen and not sure of what to do next.

Once when a reporter asked Marshal why he smiled less than his earlier days when he was so jovial, he responded without hesitation that the new responsibilities were draining him completely and it was his job to do his job. The passionate mission of transforming a large company had slowly changed into a dry job for him.

When the media starts taking excessive interest in a company for reasons beyond normal business reporting, it distracts the employees the most. They become part of the story unwillingly. Creative Tech was going through a similar experience. Every internal letter that Marshal used to write to his employees made way to the national press and got reported. Then the media analysts would create more gossip around the same.

Satvik asked Ajesh, "Do you think Marshal will be able to turnaround the company and succeed?"

Ajesh said, "Now I think he is more worried about his own survival in the organization. When he was hired as the CEO, he had complete freedom to say and do what he wanted. He was the ray of hope for everyone. He set goals. He provided directions and motivated his team to move ahead. Now three years down the line, everyone is asking him only questions and creating doubts. His honeymoon period is long over; now he has to only talk of results."

"It is not that he is not trying. He is trying to be successful at Creative Tech. Sometimes I feel he is trapped in the situation," Satvik said.

Things were surely not going well for Marshal. At the same time, two of his senior vice presidents announced resignations. One of them Michael Smith was hired by Marshal as a visionary technologist who was mandated to create high value products. He was offered a two million dollar salary – a 'trophy hire' from Silicon Valley. He was instrumental for the success of Creative Tech transformation.

"Is the ship sinking, that even his close associates have lost faith in him?" Satvik asked Ajesh.

"The corporate set up is equally cruel to everyone. It does not even spare its CEO when the going gets tough."

Though Satvik did not like many of the policies of Marshal, he did not want him to fail midway. Marshal had at least shown the right intent of transforming the company. He understood the outside environment better.

The Fourth Industrial Revolution

Vikas meanwhile had made some progress on his startup ideas though his newly launched startup was struggling for resources. He along with his small team had been creating a mobile based solution that could help people in the remote villages who were not well educated. The key part of his proposition was to provide the common utility services in the local language with voice interface. This ensured that even folks who were illiterate could transact using the application. It was a poor man's Alexa in a crude sense, but Vikas could see the direct impact of this offering. The service providers were never able to reach this segment due to high cost of distribution and little margin. It was a low hanging fruit.

Satvik told Vikas, "I can tell you for sure that had anyone in Creative Tech even thought of creating products for people in remote towns and villages, he would have been shot down at the first instance itself."

Vikas agreed, "Precisely, this is the reason that large companies are talking about the digital disruption all the time, but real ideas are coming from the smaller startups, because they are grounded. They look at solving a specific problem for a limited set up of people. Most importantly, they are willing to experiment and ready to accept the failure."

Satvik said, "A bad idea that results in the waste of time and resources is one of the most dreaded things in large organizations. Heads roll if the ideas fail. So one has to be absolutely confident of the proposal before presenting it for approval. This creates an environment where too many experiments are not encouraged, especially risky ones. The large corporates are inherently designed for success and they punish failures severely."

Vikas responded, "It is also true that a company like Creative Tech has a large customer base, an existing business to support and a brand reputation – they would never risk a product that has even a small chance of failure. The impact on the current business will be far too much. They will always be conservative in experimentation."

"This is the reason that large organizations are looking for acquisition of startups for new ideas and innovations. So in the digital age, finding new problems and solving them will come primarily from smaller companies and startups. Does it mean that large organization like Creative Tech will become irrelevant?" Satvik asked Vikas.

Vikas said, "No, not at all. Large organizations like Creative Tech can help create an ecosystem of startups where they can collaborate with each other. Though the startups have a distinct advantage on idea creation and experimentation, they get seriously constrained when they have to scale them up."

"I agree that large organizations and startups can complement each other to their benefit. Both the set ups have their distinct natural advantages and they need not compete with each other."

Vikas said, "Some organizations that are successfully riding the digital wave are precisely the ones that are able to create an ecosystem where different small organizations and startups can connect with each other. Amazon is an example of that and they are growing like anything. The same disruption that is threatening the existence of companies like Creative Tech, has become a natural advantage for Amazon."

Both Vikas and Satvik agreed that engaging with startups was a good idea. Satvik thought he would share this with Marshal when he got the next opportunity. This required change in the current team structure and processes, but it was an excellent idea to work with them to generate new ideas, especially in the digital space. Creative Tech could play the role of an incubator where they could curate ideas and pick the most relevant ones for the market. Though it did not immediately create a big revenue opportunity, this would help the organization to be relevant in the space of digital innovation.

Another thought Satvik gathered from the conversation with Vikas was that the large centralized organization would eventually become rigid and unviable in the new digital age. The new set up would be something like going back to the pre-industrial revolution age when smaller entrepreneurs were the norm. With the invention of large machines that could produce in multiples, the organizations became more centralized. The workforce became more structured with time with large scale deployments. Smaller firms and cottage industries lacked the resources to mass produce goods and services. This changed the society and the communities. Those who adopted them well became prosperous in the modern age.

The digital revolution was creating a similar change, but the other way round. Once again, the smaller companies and startups were getting empowered to create the new age products and services. With cloud, mobility and open source tools today, any individual can imagine and drive innovations. They can disrupt large organizations that are constrained by their own set up. The digital revolution has empowered the smaller entities to an extent that it can be called the Fourth Industrial Revolution. It will change the model of employment as well. Instead of few large organizations employing hundreds of thousands of people, eventually it will be scores of people, each employed by hundreds of thousands of such organizations.

The universities will train their students not on how to get employment with large factories, but how to self-create startups. It was already happening. Some universities were actively running incubation cells and encouraging the students to come up with new ideas.

Their discussion quickly moved to the fundamental reason behind the digital disruption – 'Artificial Intelligence'.

Vikas explained, "There is a fundamental change happening now in this area. Automation and AI have been in existence since quite some time in some or the other form (Artificial Neural Network was discovered in 1950s). There have been waves of incremental advancements. But this time the changes were different from the past."

This time AI was disrupting the disruptors of the last decade – companies like Creative Tech.

Technology has been the biggest disruptor in the last few decades. It has amplified human potential and freed up our times from mundane repetitive activities. Today one doesn't need to visit a bank to withdraw money, then go to every bill payment office, fill-in the receipts and pay. We have designed IT applications for them that can take care of these things online. We only have to manage those applications through sophisticated tools.

In essence, the applications were the extended arms of people who replaced physical work, but the brain functions still resided with the managers, and that was still a lot of work.

This volume of work was so high that an entire industry of cost-effective outsourcing flourished in the new flat world. The new age AI is about replacing those who create, support and enhance those applications – we don't need a huge army of outsourcing and support specialists, software maintenance team and even the future IT developers.

The advantage with AI is – all work can be additive. So a computer doctor will soon have more knowledge than any living doctor and that will keep getting enhanced with time. Today, one has to spend lakhs of rupees and years of studies to become a doctor and at the end, you get what, just one doctor. For another person to be a doctor, the whole exercise has to be repeated. If we need thousands of doctors, it needs to be repeated thousands of times. A computer doctor on the contrary is a one-time investment and you can replicate as many at zero cost.

AI innovations are at the threshold of significantly amplifying our day to day lives in all respects. The increased adoption of cloud, unlimited computational power and the network effect will surely help us increase quality of life all across. It will also create new avenues and some specialized high end jobs, but at the same time, it will render most of the operational and managerial jobs redundant.

"This also explains why many countries of late have been toying with the idea of universal basic income," Satvik replied. "There may not be enough jobs even as the countries get richer and more productive. Just as we don't need everyone to work in agriculture to create enough food for everyone, not everyone needs to work for the world's prosperity!"

Vikas responded, "That is true, this fourth industrial revolution will have a social impact much beyond a company like Creative Tech. Just like the industrial revolution created societal norms and cities, the digital revolution will change the way we relate to our work lives. All of us today derive our identity from the work we do; it gives meaning to our lives, a purpose however futile it may be. Imagine if that nine-hour long work that people at Creative Tech do, did not exist. There would be another challenge for the society to meaningfully engage everyone."

The discussions had suddenly gone beyond the context of Creative Tech up to the social set ups and human motivations in lives. Satvik was impressed with Vikas's changed perspective.

Company Politics

The media was constantly targeting Marshal and Creative Tech since the last few months and Marshal was somehow getting used to ignoring that. However, this particular one was so damaging that Marshal could not hold himself.

'Creative Tech's CEO accused of misusing company resources.' The headline was scathing.

The content of the article was even more damaging. It mentioned in detail how Marshal had exploited company resources for personal benefits. It mentioned with exact dates the list of his holidays, hiring of personal jets and excessive expenses on things like personal security.

'As part of an internal audit at Creative Tech, it was discovered that Marshal had incurred 50 lakh rupees expenses for his annual holidays with his family in Rome. Though it was a personal trip, the expenses of it were borne by Creative Tech on his insistence. It also included the personal jet hiring charges.'

This was reported in *The Business Headlines* on their front page.

The article then raised questions about the high salary that Marshal was getting, while there were salary freezes and layoffs happening at the junior staff levels. The article mentioned that Marshal had not been able to show any measurable financial improvement for Creative Tech.

The media article was definitely a hit job on Marshal, but he was angrier with the fact that someone within his close circle was feeding some motivated information for sure. The article was an exaggeration, just to make him look bad. Marshal was sure that many people within his executive team might have been upset with some of his decisions, but he never thought they would target him like this.

"I know who that person could be," Marshal told Monica. "It is the handiwork of Rajendran."

"The current COO of Creative Tech? I can't believe that," replied Monica.

"He was one of the internal candidates considered for the CEO post, but was finally rejected. He has support of some old employees. He has been behaving funny of late," Marshal replied.

"How can you be so sure about it?"

"The audit report was known to very few people. Someone has surely leaked it deliberately," replied Marshal.

Marshal was not revengeful in general, but he decided that if he let it go unnoticed, it would only increase with time. He had to punish this behaviour. For the first time, he felt insecure in his own office.

He called up Rajendran. Though it was 11 p.m. in India, Marshal could not let this incident fester anymore. Not even for one more day.

"Rajendran, did you read the *Business Headlines* report today? It has malicious content about the audit in the company and the CEO misusing the company funds," Marshal tried to say calmly.

"This is really unfortunate. This gives one more opportunity to the media to gossip about the company. I tell you, it is not helping anyone," Rajendran replied.

"I think it is a deliberate hit job, someone in the company is trying to throw me out by maligning me. Who else knew about the audit? How did the media get to know about it?"

"I have no idea. In this large organization, there are people who have some media contacts. These incidents have happened in the past as well," Rajendran replied.

"I want the emails and phone details of all the audit team members investigated. I want to find that idiot in the next twenty-four hours and fire him from the organization for playing with jobs of thousands of people who work at Creative Tech." Now Marshal was unable to hold back his anger.

"We can track the official mails, but I am sure this person would not have sent this information using his official mail id," Rajendran responded.

"Okay, then sift through their personal mail ids and phone details. If they have sent the mail during office hours, we will surely have some leads to investigate. Call the information security guy now and explain to him that this is urgent. We can hire an external detective agency to find out who from our company has spoken to the media," Marshal ordered Rajendran.

Rajendran knew that this would not only be unethical, but also possibly break company policies. All through the nitty-gritties of his role as a COO, he always ensured to be on the right side of rules and policies. He was a devout spiritual person who believed that karma always comes back to haunt us if we do something wrong.

Rajendran replied, "Marshal, any such move can backfire. We are already in the news for wrong reasons."

Marshal took it as a 'no' to follow his instructions. This further confirmed his suspicion that it was Rajendran who was behind this reportage.

Next moment, Marshal called Srinivasan, the chairman of the board. Srinivasan did not pick up the call. Marshal called him thrice in vain.

"Can't this wait till tomorrow morning?" Srinivasan was definitely not happy at this late night disturbance.

"I am sorry Srini, but I think we have a crisis at Creative Tech. Someone in my office is leaking misleading information to the media in order to sabotage Creative Tech."

"How can you be sure about the person?"

"I am sure it is Rajendran. I just spoke to him now. He refused to carry out any investigation in this matter," Marshal replied confidently.

"Rajendran had been a long timer in Creative Tech. He will not do anything to harm the foundation of the company."

"He already has. I can't work with him in this atmosphere of mistrust."

"So what are you suggesting?"

"Creative Tech needs to fire its COO Rajendran with immediate effect," Marshal said confidently.

"On what basis?"

"I will work that out with him. He has to leave, that is the only condition. You and the board have to choose between me and him."

Next, Marshal called Ronald, the legal counsel of Creative Tech and explained what he wanted in no uncertain terms.

"I just want him to keep his mouth shut from now onwards."

Ronald had a clear mandate from Marshal – to get rid of Rajendran as soon as possible, at whatever terms.

He called Rajendran, "Marshal has lost trust in you and your position becomes untenable in Creative Tech. He has spoken to Srinivasan, our chairman, and also got his concurrence."

"This company belongs to me as much as to Marshal. In fact, I have spent a longer time here," Rajendran retorted.

"That does not matter. The CEO has the prerogative to choose his team," Ronald added.

"If he thinks that he can just bulldoze me due to my differences with him, he may be wrong. I can call for a press conference and explain my position to everyone," Rajendran raised his voice.

"Have you heard of a gun that fires several bullets in different directions at the same time? Whichever direction you point that, one of the bullets is going to hit you. The media is that gun," explained Ronald.

"But Marshal has to give me a justifiable reason."

"He is saying that the chemistry with you does not work."

"See, it is not wise to make it dirty. It will be lose-lose for you. Marshal and the media will exaggerate. In the end, the company will suffer. It will be better if we find an honorable exit for you, while at the same time compensate you adequately," Ronald said.

The word compensate hit Rajendran hard.

"Are you trying to buy my silence by paying me money? Are you bribing me?"

"It is a common practice in an American company for executive level send offs," Ronald replied.

"But what if I don't want that severance package?" Rajendran smelled something fishy about it.

"Then be ready to see a headline tomorrow that the COO has been fired for underperformance," Marshal had told Ronald to make sure that Rajendran accepted the severance package.

"We are paying you something like one million dollars," Ronald said.

"But, no one has ever been paid severance package. The board and the shareholders will question that," Rajendran said.

"I will manage that. The only condition is that you will have to sign a 'non-repudiation agreement' with Creative Tech."

"I have never heard about any such agreement," Rajendran replied wiping the drops of sweat from his forehead.

"Nothing to worry, it is a one page agreement that says you will never talk about any incident of Creative Tech or their management in public or private. Similarly, Creative Tech will also reciprocate."

Rajendran was very particular about probity in his personal life. However, one thing he cared for equally was his public reputation. A newspaper report on his underperformance would be devastating for his long corporate life. He had just a few years of his work life left – he wanted an honorable exit.

"Okay, as you wish. I will sign the agreement."

Rajendran kept telling himself, "Do I still have a chance to redeem my karma?"

In the next board meeting, Marshal informed that Rajendran had decided to leave Creative Tech to pursue his personal interests. The company had to pay him a severance package in line with new executive compensation policies. Some board members raised the question on the amount, but Srinivasan said it was the day-to-day working of the company. The board was obviously not happy with this, but Marshal did not give them an option. The board's stakes were higher on Marshal; they eventually had to toe his line.

Rajendran was replaced with Robert as the new COO of Creative Tech in US. With this change, even the second most significant company position was moved out of India.

Satvik knew Robert as he was his manager for some time. Robert had little capability to be a visionary leader, leave aside steering the company to success. Satvik realized Marshal needed someone whom he could trust. He could probably live with a bit of incompetence, but not with someone who was untrustworthy.

In Marshal's journey, if there was unflinching support, it was from the chairman and the board. From time to time, they came up with strongest supporting statements for Marshal. It was the board after all that had selected Marshal.

The accusation of impropriety by the CEO was difficult to get all out support from the board though. The office politics was slowly seeping into the boardroom. There was an increasing thought process building up that Marshal was taking the company down the wrong path. During some of the board meetings, Marshal was being asked some uncomfortable questions.

Marshal wondered about his three year journey in the organization. The euphoria of his initial days had gone. When he had joined Creative Tech, he could speak for hours on the new digital technologies and the opportunities that they brought to all the employees. Now, three years down the line, even though he was more familiar with the organization, his enthusiasm had waned. Many employees had started thinking that Marshal was part of the problem that he was trying to solve.

To Quit or not to Quit

Ajesh had left Creative Tech three months back. Satvik was not surprised. Ajesh always looked for the right ship to jump to. His networks and LinkedIn connections always kept him ahead of the curve. Satvik was curious to meet him, not only to tell him about the incidents at Creative Tech, but also to know how Ajesh was doing.

"What role have you joined the new company as?" Satvik asked him.

"A data scientist."

"But you were a cloud architect in Creative Tech, weren't you?"

"Yes, but cloud was the buzzword three years back, today everyone is talking about machine learning and statistical programming."

"Though I have stopped programming now, I never heard of statistical programming as a term. Is it a new technology?"

"Okay, you have heard of structured programming, right? All that java, C, SQL languages?"

"Of course, I have. I was one of the best programmers in my early days. These are the languages that have led to the IT boom of today," Satvik replied.

"These days data scientists call them dumb programming because it does not experiment with itself. The outcome is predictable as expected from the program,"

"Let me explain further," said Ajesh.

Intelligence has three basic components:

- *Memory*
- *Computation*
- *Learnability*

While the structured programs have memory and computations, they have no learnability. The neural networks on the other hand keep on adjusting themselves till they become very good at optimizing the goal given to them.

To give you an easy example, one can buy a robodog that is pre-programmed to walk in certain way or buy a robodog that is provided with a very broad architecture of walking – that can experiment, fall and eventually learn walking based on the rewards and penalty fixed. While the first robodog can become productive early on, the performance of the second one will far outclass the first one over a period of time. Also, when the environment changes, the pre-programmed robodog will fail miserably.

"I will tell you, soon in the age of Artificial Intelligence, the structured programming that most of us are doing will be dead. Such programs can be written by our robots, because they can be codified easily."

"That is really intriguing. Your technology perspective is really futuristic. I am also amazed by your ability to manage your professional career by making the right changes," replied Satvik.

"Our corporate life is like a leaf in the river. The leaf does not try to control the flow or its direction, nor does it bother about them, it just floats. You have to search for stability in the dynamic equilibrium," replied Ajesh.

Soon after, Ajesh zoomed off in his newly purchased BMW. As he waved goodbye, it got Satvik thinking about where he had gone wrong. Was stability and predictability really an elusive term in today's corporate life?

Meanwhile, there was a long mail from Marshal to all the Creative Tech employees.

From: Marshal Scott
To: All Staff of Creative Tech

Friends,

As we close this year on a festive note, I want to celebrate our achievements as a team. While we are still in the midst of exciting transformation, we have few milestones to celebrate. We have been able to increase revenue from our newly created digital practice by almost three times. Our BITS practice has grown well since we started it a year back. Most of our clients have admired the progress we have made in automation and use of AI.

While we are making good progress on the business side, there are also some unpleasant noise in the media and informal conversations. Many of these have malicious intent and do not have any truth behind them. Creative Tech will continue to lead the software industry as it has done in the past.

I request all the staff members to stay focused on the business outcomes and not get diverted by media reports.

Best,
M

For a moment Satvik pitied Marshal. When the CEO of the organization starts writing to his own employees enumerating the good things that he has done during his tenure, it is almost certain that he is under tremendous pressure. When Marshal joined Creative Tech as CEO, his first fault was with the employees; as an embattled CEO his last recourse was the employees now.

Also, this time there was no talk of the 10 billion target that Marshal had introduced three years back. He was reconciled to the fact that the company may not reach that number in the next two years – just that he could never say that in an open letter to all the employees.

To Satvik, this letter was more like an admission that "as a CEO, I have not been up to your expectations. Please pardon me and forgive my mistakes. Let us all move on."

While Creative Tech was still under transformational turmoil, Vikas was gaining momentum with his startup. He had increased his team size to more than a hundred people and had got good funding from key investors. At one point of time, Satvik wondered if it could be a good decision to join Vikas's company.

"If you are perturbed with the instability in Creative Tech and looking for a less turbulent job, let me tell you that my startup has ten times more instability. You are worried about the long term career in the organization, for me these worries are as immediate as next month's bills. It will never give you any better peace of mind. It is just that I have gone beyond those worries some time back," Vikas told Satvik.

"But I read so many good things about your startup. There is positivity and enthusiasm in the team. You are expanding and don't seem to be having all the problems that Creative Tech has," Satvik responded.

"See Satvik, for all the good news that you read, there is a dark side of a startup as well. There is a selection bias in the news

SUNIL MISHRA

reporting. They only report the successful cases. For every success, there are scores of startups that are closing down every other day. The only thing is that many of them don't give up – they don't stop at the failures. The key to success is also to fail early and switch tracks."

Perhaps Vikas was right. Satvik was looking at startups for the wrong reasons – for getting rid of his current problems at Creative Tech. But the startups had more problems in reality. They had existential threats every other day.

"Have you seen the vacation photographs of your friend, Ajesh? They went for a fifteen-day Europe tour," Neeraja asked Satvik.

"I read an article today that psychologists are warning everyone to stay away from Facebook. These days Facebook is making people more discontent and unhappy with their own lives," Satvik responded.

"Nice diversion tactic, but both of you worked in the same company at a similar position. How is it that he is able to afford such expenses while we are still dreaming about it?" Neeraja asked.

"How ironical," Satvik thought. While he was thinking of taking the plunge, his wife was still expecting more from his current job. "What will she do if I really told her about what I discussed with Vikas today," he wondered.

"Unfortunately, the lure of the monthly salary is the helplessness that forces most of us to work," Satvik replied.

"Honey, if you don't get monthly salaries, all this inspirational talk will sound hollow," cautioned Neeraja.

"This is the real problem, our perennial insistence on predictability. From the start of the education system early on, we aim for stability," replied Satvik.

"I hope you are reading the right books and don't plan to do something stupid. Don't count on me in that case." Neeraja was increasingly worried about the way Satvik had been talking of late.

Satvik was not willing to take the plunge into the world of startups. He was wedded to the monthly salary. He could not gather enough courage to step into the unchartered territory. The fact was that in some corner of his heart, his corporate career ambition was still very much alive. He was expecting his next promotion someday, to grow in Creative Tech.

The Whistleblower

The media was having a field day with juicier stories on Creative Tech. Now even the board was an active player as some of the stories started blaming the chairman and the other board members. In all these events, the regulators were getting concerned whether the governance standards were being upheld.

Amongst all this turmoil, suddenly there was a whistleblower letter to the regulator, the board and the key shareholders.

From: A Creative Tech well wisher
To: SEBI, Creative Tech Board Members, Shareholders

Sub: Investigation of recent acquisitions by Creative Tech

Dear Creative Tech Stakeholders,

I want to bring to your attention the recent acquisition of Vcoins – a virtual currency based startup. This proposal was brought up a few months back. It was primarily rejected by everyone in the decision committee as it was in a speculative field, not yet approved by the legal authorities.

Subsequently, due to the insistence of Marshal, this proposal was again taken up where he impressed upon the benefits of this transaction. The committee had to reconsider the decision and eventually a resolution was passed reversing the earlier decision.

Now it has come to my notice from very confirmed sources that Marshal's wife Monica is one of the investors in Vcoin. This makes Marshal directly responsible for non-disclosure of key information regarding conflict of interest. This information was brought up to the notice of Srinivasan and some of the other board members. However, they failed to act due to reasons best known to them.

I request SEBI to investigate the matter and take appropriate action. This is a clear violation of sound governance principles by the Creative Tech management and the board.

Regards

The chairman of the board was in a fix. It was direct indictment on the board along with Marshal. Srinivasan confronted Marshal.

"The whistleblower has raised a conflict of interest issue for Vcoin acquisition."

"That whistleblower is none other than Rajendran. He is still not done with his smear campaign. He was damaging Creative Tech with his rumours and propaganda all the while," Marshal responded.

"He has raised a direct charge about your involvement in the acquisition," the chairman persisted with the question.

"If you really believe a liar outgoing COO more that the current CEO, you are free to carry out an independent investigation," Marshal responded.

The chairman thought, Marshal was trying to pre-empt an action. There was no point in discussing this further.

An independent agency was hired by the board to investigate not only Vcoin, but all the acquisitions by the new CEO. Marshal took it as a personal affront from the chairman and the board. At once, he wanted to just drop all his responsibilities and move on. He had had enough of this nonsense, he thought. However, leaving the organization when there was an accusation would increase the suspicions from his detractors. He allowed the board to move ahead with the enquiry.

There was a six-week enquiry by the agency. At the end of six weeks, a confidential report was submitted to the board. It essentially highlighted some lapses in procedure and governance, but stopped short of indicting any individual for the wrongdoing. The board was relieved. The last thing they wanted was to deal with an expected crisis due to this investigation. Though there was a demand to make the entire report public, the board was strictly against washing dirty linen in public. Even if there was a small lapse somewhere, this might open a floodgate of litigations and lawsuits that could take the company down. The chairman put a brave face and stood by the report and defended his CEO. It was the most practical approach under prevailing conditions at Creative Tech.

"How can an organization hire an agency to investigate itself? And give it a clean chit in the end? How credible can that be?" some of the media reports raised concern on governance.

Some stakeholders also raised doubts on the board that it was not competent enough to control a CEO who spoke a tech language. The board members however defended the broad actions of Marshal. These transactions left everyone in Creative Tech with something to lose.

The 13th quarterly result of the company was not very rosy. When Marshal presented it to his board for approval, he had to face a barrage of questions.

"Marshal, at this rate, will we be anywhere be close to our 10 billion target?" one of the board members asked.

"We are doing our best. The 10 billion target was more of an aspiration. We will surely achieve that someday. It is a direction that is important," Marshal responded.

"Marshal, how will you react if we say that you will get your performance bonus someday, not this year?"

Marshal was upset. His entire vision and work was at scrutiny. He said the board was free to take decisions based on what it deemed fit. He was not in a mood to discuss this. He left the board meeting in a huff.

The results were announced, but Marshal was conspicuous by his absence.

The next day, there were headlines in the newspapers.

'Creative Tech punishes its CEO by cutting down 80% of the variable pay.'

The media had already declared the verdict – the CEO had failed. It was only a matter of time now.

Marshal wished he had not taken this job. He informed his secretary that he would not be reachable for the next few days as he had to attend to a personal emergency. He excused himself from all the meetings.

Marshal's wife Monica was more concerned about this sudden change of behaviour.

"You seem to be so stressed these days. Is everything alright at Creative Tech?" she asked.

"I did not sign up for this," Marshal responded.

"Why don't you resign and move on to some other job? I am sure you will find a good one," Monica suggested gently.

"I have to redeem myself before I quit," Marshal was more determined to stay the course than Monica imagined.

CEO's Act 4

Satvik got a note from the CEO office regarding another business review. This time there was no Vikas. He could be in the direct line of fire, Satvik thought. Only a miracle could save his job.

Satvik went to Marshal's office one more time, expecting to wait for long hours. He had made a mental map of the entire conversation based on his previous experiences, "I would plead guilty in the very first instance. I would not question any new target that Marshal gives me and my team. Since I have still not made much progress in the digital, I would just accept my mistakes."

To his surprise, Satvik did not have to wait for Marshal. He called him into his meeting room on time.

"Nice seeing you, Satvik, after a long time. How you have been doing?" Marshal greeted him warmly.

"Thank you Marshal, I am doing fine."

"I see, your unit has done quite well this year," Marshal told Satvik. Initially Satvik thought, Marshal was just being sarcastic.

"I know Marshal, you may not be happy with our performance in the current cycle, but let me assure you, we will do our best to match-up the three targets you gave last time," Satvik pleaded virtually.

"No, Satvik I really mean it. Your team has improved the revenue by 30% and most of it is from emerging technology areas in digital, our focus area of BITS," Marshal added further.

"Really?" Satvik still could not believe it. He looked at the worksheet that Marshal was looking at. It indeed showed improved numbers.

But I have not done anything significantly different, so I am not sure how this new numbers have been arrived at, Satvik thought. He suddenly felt like a student who thought he had failed in the exam but found his name among the toppers. Satvik did not know how to react to the situation.

Satvik looked at the numbers again. It did not match his own calculations. He was wondering if he was missing something. Satvik got to the bottom of the sheet where list of accounts were mentioned. One of them was Indian Bank.

"Marshal, the revenue from Indian Bank can't be recognized in this quarter, as it is disputed. The bank has not yet signed-off on the milestone."

"In software licence, we should recognize the revenue at the time of delivery of the licence key, not the client sign-off. This is the international practice," Marshal replied.

"But what if the bank does not pay us the amount tomorrow?"

A closer observation by Satvik revealed that Marshal had recently triggered a change in the revenue recognition policy. Creative Tech had been very conservative in reporting revenues earlier. The licence revenue could be recognized in the company book only after successful completion of the project and a sign-off from the client. Also, in case of any dispute, the entire amount was disclosed separately as provision.

Marshal mentioned it was an old practice. As per the new norms, the revenue could be recognized at the time of signing of the contract. This made many of their long running projects suddenly add up to the unit numbers. Satvik was a great performer without even doing anything knowingly.

Marshal also congratulated him saying that most of Satvik's revenue had been categorized as the digital. This was the icing on the cake. For the last many years, Satvik had struggled to understand what was digital, and how this could relate to his work. Here he got a reward on the platter.

Satvik realized this was no longer his review. It was Marshal's. He was not rewarding Satvik, but making him a partner in his act. Marshal was trying desperately to save his own standing. He wanted to prove his success.

"Satvik, you have led one of the excellent performing units in Creative Tech. I think you will be happy to know that we have created a position for you in our US office. I am sure you would look forward to this opportunity." Marshal looked at Satvik's reaction.

Satvik could not believe his ears. He pinched himself to check if he was not dreaming. When he had walked into Marshal's room that day, he was full of apprehension. He had thought it could be his last day at Creative Tech. Here he was getting rewarded with the American dream – something Ajesh tried so hard for, but could not succeed. For once he had beaten Ajesh, Satvik thought. He imagined himself sitting in the Palo Alto office next to the CEO's office. He thought of throwing a grand party where he would call both Vikas and Ajesh.

There was silence in the room for some time, till the office boy walked up to Satvik and asked, "Coffee or tea?"

"Tea without sugar," responded Satvik.

Marshal picked up the sheet that Satvik had brought.

"Satvik, please rework the numbers as per our discussion and submit them to the unit finance by today. We have to close the book for this quarterly result."

"But I don't agree with these numbers; they are definitely not correct," Satvik said.

"When the company has to transform, it will change in everything, including the way revenue is recognized and reported," Marshal was insistent.

"It will be wrong on my part to misrepresent data just to make it look better. It will be called window dressing, a kind of financial engineering to boost revenue and profits," Satvik replied.

"All the units have revised their numbers accordingly. You will have to do the same," Marshal said.

"Please don't force me to do this, Marshal. You can always override me and go ahead."

"It has to be done as part of the regular finance reporting. Each program manager has to submit the same. If I override it, it will need to be approved by the audit committee." Marshal was insistent once again.

Through thick and thin at Creative Tech, Satvik had chugged along the company. For him, employment was long term proposition that he valued, but there was one more thing that he valued even more – integrity. Satvik didn't know the dictionary definition of integrity or the business equivalence of the same, but something inside him said no. He froze for a few minutes, just to overcome his fear of losing his job. The lure of American dream also flashed again.

"Satvik, in a corporate situation, sometimes we don't have a choice. We have to go by whatever seems most practical," Marshal said.

"No Marshal, it may not be a correct observation, we all have choices all the time, more so in our corporate lives."

And Satvik walked out of the room.

Satvik had made the decision in a state of high anxiety. A review that started with fear and turned into applause, finally ended in his resignation. Satvik did not repent though. Marshal was manipulating Satvik for values that were very dear to him.

Sudden departures had become quite common in the last couple of years, Satvik was just another one. Satvik joined the long list of digital transformation martyrs in Creative Tech.

Soon after leaving Creative Tech, Satvik met Vikas.

"He offered you a position in the US in his office? You denied that and instead ended up resigning from the company? This is a very weird turn of events." Vikas could not believe it.

"This is called perfect self-destruction. You managed to convert your reward into your nemesis. These opportunities do not come every day – you need to understand that."

"But, I did not agree with what Marshal was doing; it was wrong," Satvik replied.

"So what happened after you left? Did the next guy not sign-off the numbers? Did your refusal change the outcome that Marshal wanted?"

"Do you think the hangman agrees with the decision of executing a person? He does it because he thinks it is his job to do what he is told. In corporate life, we all become hangmen at times; we just do it," Vikas added.

Satvik was already feeling low, and this discourse from Vikas was making him realize the enormity of his decision.

"Have you found another job?" Vikas asked, after Satvik was quiet for some time.

"How could I? It was a spontaneous decision. I did not even know about this outcome when I went to Marshal for the review," Satvik replied.

"You have done a stupid thing," Vikas told Satvik. "You know how difficult it is to find another job these days at our level of experience?"

Vikas was right. Satvik knew from his own experience how difficult it was for senior level hiring in his own company. Managers like Satvik used to be called 'overhead' – something that does not add value, but has high cost.

"In a corporate set up, you should keep your emotions aside," he advised Satvik.

"The instant thoughtless decision provoked by anger can virtually end your professional career. What will you tell your other prospective employers if you can't find a job in the next few months? How will you explain the gap in experience?" Vikas explained further.

Now Satvik was slowly beginning to understand the practical impact of his own decision. It was an emotional decision that could be suicidal.

"How could you have planned it better?" Satvik asked Vikas.

"Do you think Ajesh left Creative Tech out of his own choice? No, but he planned it well. In your professional life, you need to be vigilant of what is happening around you. Sometimes that is more important than your own performance. You landed up in the same situation as me, even though I was fired while you had an option," Vikas told Satvik.

"See, in any corporate career, especially in IT, there are four distinct phases and you need to ride them well to reach the top."

"The starting phase is Engineer/consultant – when you start your corporate career fresh from the college, you are like a horse – the faster you run, more energy you put in, you will excel in your work. This is a phase of brute force. You just need to work hard.

"*You are mainly an individual contributor in this phase. If you manage yourself well, you will be the star performer in the initial four-five years of your career.*

"*The second phase is client/project manager – all of us ultimately work for a client, more so in IT. This is a phase when all that matters is how well you manage client deliveries and expectations. Here it is fine balance of skill – managing your own team and clients. This is less of individual contribution and more of team play.*

"*Though it is a progression of a hardworking doer phase, the key success factors are no longer the same. You need to be good in soft skills more than the subject matter. You would typically manage a project in this phase. Your key stakeholders are the clients who decide your success or failure.*

"*The third phase is portfolio manager/principals – In this phase you are already in your thirties and have managed few projects successfully. Your key work would be to manage a portfolio of disparate projects on an ongoing basis. Since it is a portfolio of projects, all of them would not be equally great projects. There will be bad projects and it depends how you keep your CEO happy with the positive perception.*

"*In this phase, your key stakeholders are no longer clients or individual teams. Your entire focus is on managing your own boss. This is also a most crowded space and there are many in waiting line here. Any slip and there will be another replacement.*

"*You, me, Ajesh, all fall in this bracket currently. It did not matter how well we did in our portfolio, all that mattered was what Marshal thought of us. He always had people in the waiting line. You also have to be most vigilant in this phase and manage the corporate politics. Ajesh got to know that Marshal was hiring for the position of Digital Architecture Head, his prevailing designation in Creative Tech, before he left. He met me that time and told me probably sooner or later he would be on the chopping block. He started looking out for a job and finally got one after three months. If you want to be successful in corporate life, you have to be vigilant like Ajesh.*

"The final stage in the corporate hierarchy is CEO/Partner – You need to go through all the previous three phases only to realize that the key success factors in this phase are entirely different. You would work for the shareholders now who are represented by the board. The set up will reward you not based on how popular you are among your employees, but how much dividends you are paying to the shareholders or how has the market capitalization improved.

"This explains why the CEOs beyond a point do not bother about employee satisfaction even when it is sometimes problematic. If you observe carefully, Marshal's three goals are all aligned to the shareholder's profit maximization. He also knows that some of these are conflicting, like, a cost cutting by laying off employees will eventually hurt the morale of the employees.

"It also depends on how the CEO looks at long term vs short term objectives. If there is excessive focus on the quarterly performance, rest assured that the CEO will continue to be cut throat in implementing his policies."

Satvik realized Vikas had some real insights into corporate life, even though he could not ride it well. He was also right in describing these four phases so distinctly and it explained well why the same person was not equally successful in the different phases. Someone could be a great consultant with all the knowledge, but may perform poorly while managing client projects or managing his or her own boss as a portfolio head.

"How do these career phases get impacted by digital transformation that is currently underway in Creative Tech?" Satvik asked Vikas.

"The digital disruption has definitely changed some of these phases. For example, if you have a great idea, you can surely create a product with a very small team and offer it to large number of customers directly. It has helped the people in earlier phases," Vikas responded.

"The most impacted layer because of these digital disruptions is people in the portfolio manager level. Our job of managing the expectation of our CEO was difficult already, now with changing priorities by Marshal and direct impact of his decisions, we are even more vulnerable."

"Do you think I could have handled the situation better? Was there any future for me in Creative Tech?" Satvik asked Vikas.

"I explain this by my thumb rule called 'Trust-Competency matrix," Vikas responded.

"You know Satvik, in a competitive corporate set up at the senior level, the leader categorizes people on a two by two matrix – 'my man' and 'competent man'. Even though it does not happen explicitly, it happens in the mind of your boss. It has huge implications on your career. At every point in time, you should evaluate which quadrant you belong to in this matrix," Vikas explained further.

"What does it mean to be in any specific quadrant? What are the implications?" Satvik asked further.

"Let me explain. If the leader puts you in 'not my man' and 'not competent' category – rest assured, you will fall off soon without any hope. If you are put in the 'not my man' but 'competent' category – you will be watched for, but will never grow much. Here, if you present too much resistance, you could jeopardize your career. If the leader puts you in the 'my man' but 'not competent' category, you will be put for all and sundry work, but your job will be probably safe. For very few, the leader categorizes them in the 'my man' and 'competent' category – such people fly higher in the corporate career. Keep in mind, to grow in the corporate set up, you need both the trust of your bosses as well as competency."

"I probably fell in the 'competent' but 'not my man' category since sometimes I opposed Marshal's policies," Satvik concluded.

This argument gave Satvik some relief that he could well have been a victim of circumstances and possibly he could forgive himself for the sudden emotional decision of leaving Creative Tech.

"There are some values that all of us find very dear to our heart and we don't want to compromise. The financial reporting that Marshal insisted was probably one such thing. According to me, it was fraud and had to be countered. Though I regret my decision of reacting at the spur of the moment, I don't see how my decisions could have been any different even today," Satvik explained his situation.

"In corporate life, you are free to choose your fight, but be very selective of the conflict where you are willing to martyr yourself. It is foolish to confront your CEO about a topic that threatens his own existence. It is not about right or wrong; it is about practicality."

Just like previous times, Satvik liked the insights from Vikas. Only he wished if he could have spoken to him on this topic earlier.

Discovery of New Work
in the Digital World

Since it was a sudden exit, Satvik could not immediately find another job. He was worried that in the prevailing market situation, he was not even best prepared to compete at his level. Satvik had only known how to interview candidates and accept or reject them. He had always been an interviewer for the last many years and the thought of being an interviewee scared him.

The first task was to make an up-to-date resume. Satvik selected some of the best resume templates that he had seen last year. He kept on filling in his accomplishments for the last fifteen years.

The next task was to look for vacancies. Earlier there used to be newspapers that would advertise for open positions. Now he realized that there was no proactive way to find a job. He updated his profile on job portals and uploaded the current resume. Beyond this, there was hardly anything that Satvik could do. He recalled Ajesh telling him once, "At our level of seniority, you can't find a job, the jobs need to find you. All you can do is signal that you are available for hiring and wait for someone to call you."

Few weeks passed, nothing happened. Finally, during the fourth week, Satvik got a call from a recruitment agent.

"Sir, they need an architect in their product division. It may not be the exact match for your profile, but it is a very lucrative offer."

Satvik agreed, not that he had an option to reject. It was a good company after all.

On the day of the interview, Satvik reached the venue one hour before. He was getting ready in formals after a long time, since Creative Tech had discontinued the same in office. The tie was particularly discomforting now. He also saw several other candidates, almost twenty of them. Some were tense, some holding books and doing last minute revisions.

At this time, the HR coordinator came to the room and announced.

"We will have a short aptitude and programming test for one hour. Only selected candidates will be invited for the interview."

"But we were not told about the test," Satvik said mildly.

"It is part of our selection criteria. You should have looked up our portal."

Everyone else was quiet, only Satvik was protesting. It was becoming awkward for him, but Satvik was equally scared. What if he failed in the aptitude test? Satvik had not done any programming for the last many years. There he would definitely fail, he thought. Satvik was also not prepared to be evaluated by a bunch of young engineers whom he could not have even hired in his team at Creative Tech.

He walked out of the interview area quietly. He told the HR anchor that due to the delay, he had a conflict with another meeting and he would not attend the interview. The fact was he had developed cold feet.

During the next interview of another organization, Satvik put down his condition that he was not going to take any test, be it aptitude, programming, essay or any such damn thing.

This time, Satvik was first invited for the HR round. It was surprising because as per his understanding, the HR round was the last round of interview, and was insignificant. The HR person was usually expected to talk warmly to the candidate so that the offer was not rejected. An HR round meant that the candidate had passed the selection process.

"We have made some changes in the selection process, due to the large number of applicants for the position. We just want to screen the candidate before to save the time of panel members," the HR lady said flipping through his three-page resume and leaning back on the chair.

"Yes, that is a good idea."

"Your profile is really interesting and it fits well into our position."

"Thank you for the compliment. I am sure I will be able to add value to your organization."

"Of course, you will. Creative Tech, where you have worked earlier, is a great organization."

Satvik was relieved. Hopefully he should be able to clear this interview.

"Satvik, your resume mentions that you left Creative Tech two months back."

"Yes, madam, that is mentioned correctly."

"So it means you are currently unemployed."

The term 'unemployed' hit Satvik hard – his perennial fear had come true. He did not know how to react to that.

"Satvik, our company policies state that we can't hire people who have gaps in education or employment."

The news of layoff in the IT companies was doing the rounds already. Many companies suspected that the gap in employment could be possibly due to the layoff. This was a polite way to refuse some candidates who could have been marked as an underperformer or redundant in the previous organization.

Satvik dropped the idea of attending more interviews.

During the last few years, Satvik had just been managing things using the company resources that were given to him. He had become a manager. He needed a team to deliver results. It was seven years back that Satvik had learned the last programming language. He had stopped learning new technologies long back. He painfully realized that his skills were no longer sought after by prospective employers. Satvik needed a reboot, re-learning and probably a re-look at the remaining part of his professional career. He needed a switch and that could never come by doing more of the same things; something fundamental needed to be tweaked.

Satvik had always loved to read books. He recalled how he was an avid reader since his school days. In the last few years, Satvik had discontinued the habit, mainly due to the hectic work schedule.

That weekend, Satvik visited the nearest bookshop and bought scores of books on various subjects – from history of mankind to how to win in the digital world. He also bought various 'self-help books'. In the prevailing situation, Satvik thought that the only true friends could be books. They provided the foresight and also helped reflect on what was happening to Satvik.

Satvik thought about his early days as a child – he was so full of energy, hope and aspirations. He never felt exhausted. He had always set tough goals for himself and kept achieving them. Satvik kept changing and elevating the goals as well; it was all fun. Some people find studies burdensome, but Satvik enjoyed every bit of it because he saw a reward in them. Satvik was a learner when he was in school, during his engineering days and early days in Creative Tech. Then something happened – if he looked back at the last five years, he no longer had that hunger to learn. There were no goals for him, there were no drives.

On second thought Satvik realized, all his goals in the past were provided by the external environment. There were pre-defined objectives; he just needed to follow them diligently. Satvik was provided with a direction always. Last few years, the environment had stopped giving him cues to fix his next goals. He was lost completely. Since the experiment and fun disappeared from his work, he started bothering more about the other things. He got scared of his own job. That's when he started seeing a hostile environment everywhere, Marshal was just one such antagonist. Creative Tech seemed like a changed company, whereas in reality, it was Satvik who had changed, from being a curious ever changing learner to a skeptic who feared any change whether within or around. He had to now re-invent himself to the same boy in school who took every exam as a challenge, every game as a learning opportunity.

During the next several weeks, Satvik immersed himself in different kinds of books. To understand what was happening to him, it was important to understand what was happening around him. He read about the disrupting technologies being discussed like Blockchain, artificial intelligence, cloud and their potential for the future. He had heard about these terms in the past, but always dismissed them as being mere hypes. Satvik was so preoccupied in his work that he hardly gave it serious attention.

Reading various books, Satvik realized that what was happening in the digital disruption was unprecedented in the IT industry. For the first time, he seemed to agree with Marshal's grim assessment of Creative Tech becoming extinct if they did not proactively adapt to the forthcoming digital wave. Marshal was well informed. After all, he was well networked with various analysts, technical gurus and futurists. Two technologies in particular – Blockchain and Artificial Intelligence could be so disruptive that it could make huge proportion of current IT employees redundant.

Satvik started with Blockchain. This was an enigmatic topic; he had heard some people saying it is the next internet of our time, at the same time some had wished it off as an illegal way to transfer money using bitcoins. A more detailed study of the topic revealed to him that it was an accidental discovery that might have far reaching social consequences as well. Just like the fundamental technological changes in the past changed the way we lived our lives, the possible effect of Blockchain adoption was far reaching.

Internet was one of the most transforming inventions of our times. It allowed everyone to connect with each other easily and made information available at the click of a button. It disrupted many of the prevailing communication means like post-offices, libraries, etc.

Though the internet created an open architecture of knowledge creation and sharing, it allowed many public and private entities to monopolize the data and knowledge. The large corporations created data silos based on their reach and prowess. Few other institutions sprung up to mediate and facilitate transactions. These central institutions were keys to build trust and resolve disputes amongst various entities.

Blockchain fundamentally eliminates these central institutions and replaces them by a string of mathematical rules. Mathematics will be the central arbiter in the Blockchain world. The technology ensures that there is no single data store by any entity. The data is stored as de-centralized ledgers on a string of computers that no single entity owns. The distributed multiple copies also ensure that they can't be tempered with easily. This may have revolutionary impact everywhere, be it banks, medical records, land records, etc. This also makes the banks and central regulators virtually irrelevant because the system self-governs itself. It is based on the open technology, so the biggest disruption it can cause to will be the large banks and companies like Creative Tech who make software for the banks. People can store and transfer money without needing banks.

Now Satvik was realizing that the world was changing faster than he thought it was. Another technology area that caught his attention was the increasing adoption of Artificial Intelligence. The self-driving car example that Marshal used to provide was just one application of the same. The advancements in machine learning, natural language processing, deep learning and human like bot interface were the last frontiers in technology. Human beings feel very threatened if any machine seems to develop more intellect than them. With the industrial revolution, it was accepted that machines would be more powerful than humans physically. It was made to augment human capability of creating physical infrastructure, cars, etc. The thinking part nonetheless continued with humans.

The machine learning for the first time was breaking that barrier. A program can self-learn without needing a supervisor or programmer. A robot can watch hundreds of YouTube videos and learn how to make an omelette without being programmed for that. This unsupervised way of learning was the new element in Artificial Intelligence. What Marshal called 'ageless software' and Satvik dismissed as merely a figment of imagination, was already happening in the real world. The technological changes were more profound than they might have ever been.

Satvik planned to visit a startup hub in the city. He had visited the place once when Vikas took him there, but this time, Satvik was keener. It was a small set up where some of the teams shared space to work on their ventures.

Satvik was amazed at the energy level of the budding entrepreneurs. They were all engrossed in what they believed was a great idea to work on. Satvik met a team of four engineers who had just graduated the previous year. They were now working to create an intelligent chatbot.

"Do you know there are already chatbots available in the market?" Satvik asked, "There are big companies like Apple, Google, Amazon and Microsoft all working on this technology."

"Yes, we know," one of them responded.

"We have studied their chatbots in great detail and now we believe that our virtual assistant is more intelligent than them," another engineer standing by the side responded.

"We can demonstrate that. We know what are the functions they can't do and where they fail. Our VA can book a bus for you to Hyderabad, pay your local electricity bills, get you the cheapest taxi and also set an alarm. A Siri or Alexa can only do one of four like just setting the alarm," they proudly said.

Satvik liked their confidence. He also understood the point that this technology space was so vast that just a few organizations could never monopolize it. There was generic product development and domain specific niche product development. Smaller startups had huge advantage in the second category.

Satvik was also surprised to see that all these startups were working on the latest technologies and had access to the latest tools. Thanks to the cloud infrastructure like Amazon, they could rent hardware and software at rapid speed without much procedural delay.

Another thing that Satvik was startled to find was most of these entrepreneurs had no economic safety. They were not millionaires who had enough money to experiment. This was another myth that Satvik had lived with. He did one day want to venture out, but only when he had enough financial security. He had waited for the right time at least for the last fifteen years, and still was not ready for that. The definition of enough kept changing with time. Ironically, years of a secure job had not yet created the financial security that he wanted.

Satvik liked meeting some of those young entrepreneurs. Everyone had stories of successes and many failures. The good thing was they were working on a range of ideas. Satvik was surprised to find a team that was working on how to land a spaceship on the moon. The energy and momentum were infectious.

Satvik remembered Vikas's counsel, "Saying that one has no time to learn new things in technology is like saying one has no time to refuel his car while on a long drive."

Just like a car can't keep going on endlessly without refueling, a human mind also can't grow endlessly if one stops learning new things. It was more of a question of self-determination and willingness to learn new things that was crucial.

The CEO's Final Act

The quarterly results of Creative Tech were good this time around. The company showed an increased revenue growth. The market also noticed the rise in the digital revenue share that was reported for the first time. The share prices went up more than 10% after a long time.

Satvik knew this was just one-quarter bravado. This could not be a sustainable basis to call success of an organizational transformation, but any relief was good for Marshal, given the sustained pressure he had been in.

Although to the external world it was an excellent quarterly report, the board was not quite amused. They had many letters from the employees post the result, complaining about the change in conservative revenue recognition policy that jacked up the numbers. It was only window dressing, many alleged. The chairman accosted Marshal.

"Marshal, we were not aware that the revenue norms were changed. Any such modification requires an approval from the board as well."

"Looks like you are still not happy with the market performance. The revenue norms were outdated, extra conservative. We have only aligned it with best practices," Marshal replied.

"We are happy, but this can't be at the cost of larger governance principles," the chairman said.

"Are you hinting that there have been irregularities while reporting the results?" Marshal asked.

"This is something that we have to investigate. It has been reported by several managers from the company," the chairman said.

Something snapped inside Marshal. He walked out of the room.

"I find it really devastating – the distrust from my own employees. Here I am trying my best to show the company in good light while my own employees are trying to shoot me down. The worst thing is that now the board is also siding with them," Marshal thought.

The possibility of one more investigation by the board against Marshal was the last straw. More than the investigation, he was worried about the media coverage, as someone would surely leak this juicy news and he would be further embarrassed. The entire system had suddenly turned against him.

"Let us part ways." Marshal was done with this nonsense of being under surveillance all the time. Though it appeared to be a sudden decision to Srinivasan, for Marshal it was not. He knew he was riding a tiger and one day he was going to be eaten up by it.

Just a day later, all of a sudden, the news outlets started reporting that Marshal had resigned from Creative Tech.

In a statement to the security regulators the board said,

'Today, Marshal Scott, CEO of Creative Tech offered his resignation from the company citing personal reasons. The company thanks Marshal for contributing to the growth of Creative Tech over the last three years. The board has selected Venkata Subramaniam as interim CEO till the next selection of a CEO is completed.'

The sudden news of the CEO resigning created havoc in the stock market as the share price fell more than 15% in a single day. The conspiracy theory in the media ran aplenty – some blamed the current board for not being able to manage the expectations, some called Marshal a failure. The bigger questions were about the strategic directions that Marshal had set for Creative Tech. Almost all of them were work in progress and had reached only halfway to successful completion.

Though Marshal's resignation was a shock to most, for many other employees of Creative Tech, it was almost a matter of time. Marshal had lost energy to drive any change in the last few months. He had stopped talking about the digital disruption and transformation that he spoke so passionately when he joined the organization. It was only a question of when and not whether he would finally leave his current job.

When asked by the media, the Chairman said "Though we are fully committed to digital transformation, this time we want to hire a CEO who has good understanding of our current organization. We don't want to hire an external CEO."

The board had learned the lesson – not to rock the boat again with a rock star CEO. For the time being, Creative Tech once again got pushed into the cycle of uncertainty.

The digital turnaround was complete. It had not only ejected Satvik, Rajendran, Vikas and Ajesh out of Creative Tech, but Marshal himself was thrown out of the digital orbit. It did not spare anyone.

Monica was away for a weeklong VC fund raising event in a different city. It was so hectic that she could not even talk to Marshal during this period. When she learned about the sudden turn of events, she was surprised,

"How come the things turned so bad?"

"It became difficult to continue with the nonsense. Every day they were charging me with new allegations, the worst being that I violated the financial reporting norms. They were also trying to drag your name alongside in the Vcoin acquisition. My reputation would have been in tatters so I decided to end this charade," Marshal replied.

"I am really sorry to hear this, dear. It has been unfortunate. I believe you did your best to achieve the company objectives. You could have been pushy at times, but how can a change management ever be gentle?" Monica replied.

"I don't want to talk about it Monica, at least not now," replied Marshal.

"Sure, take care."

Monica however could not accept these sudden turn of events. She somehow felt responsible for suggesting Vcoin to Marshal which turned out to be the start of his worries. Next day morning when Marshal was reading the morning newspaper in bright sunny morning, Monica started the discussion again.

"Marshal, I know you have gone through turbulence in Creative Tech. I am keen to know how you look at this whole saga. Is there a lesson in that?"

"What is the purpose of such a lesson now, when it is all over?" Marshal asked Monica.

"The story is over, but I still want to understand why things turned the way they did. See, usually when we are operating in a context as an actor, we are so busy with the action that we forget to learn from it. The learning comes when we reflect back in a more detached way. In corporate lives, people wear masks of their roles and they get too carried away with that," Monica insisted.

On second thought, Marshal agreed that a dispassionate reflection on the incidents of last three years would bring up the lessons for future benefits.

"Marshal, looking back into the last three years' tenure, what is one thing that you repent you should not have done?" Monica asked.

"There were many things probably, but one thing I believe I should not have done was setting a target of 10 billion USD revenue unilaterally, without any buy-in from the teams. I knew it was a stretched target for the company. I wish I would have resisted the temptation to impress my board by creating a dream that was almost impossible to achieve." Marshal was candid in his reply.

"And that led to firing of many people in your team?" Monica responded.

"Possibly yes, many of my executives protested that a target like that was unachievable. At one time I thought that my executive team was a problem because they did not want to stretch themselves to aspirational goals. I thought they were becoming lazy and that led to the exit of many of my seasoned management team," Marshal added further.

"Did those aspirational targets create a negative impact instead?" Monica asked.

"They would have got the company target one fine day from the press as part of the quarterly results. They might have been caught by complete surprise. In such cases, the team would not feel challenged by the stretched target – they would have felt as if they were teased," Monica said.

"Can't agree with you more," Marshal said.

"I slowly realized that the goals I set for the company became my personal goal and the rest of the team members almost disowned them. I tried pushing the hard targets on my management team, but it did not work. Last one year, those goals started haunting me badly. The strange part was no one in the company was worried about not meeting those goals except me. In the last few months, the media used those goals to tease me. That's when it became unbearable." Marshal was quite articulate.

"I had warned you about organizational culture coming in the way of transformation. You went from a very different western cultural set up to lead a team that was predominantly Indian. In hindsight, do you think that helped in creating a bridge or it was responsible for bigger problems?" Monica asked Marshal.

"At first, I underestimated the role of organizational culture for the transformation. Since I was hired to change the basic DNA of the organization, I suspected that the existing culture was at the root of the problem. It was an easy target, but not the real one. Looking back, I can only conclude that culture is the wrong battle to start with. An organizational culture grows organically based on the circumstances and the prevailing context. It is not good or bad by itself," Marshal said.

"And when you attack the organizational culture as a newly joined CEO, you antagonize your team the most," Monica responded.

"When I gave lengthy discourse on how Silicon Valley firms were innovating in the technology area, the employees sensed at times that I was trying to lecture them on the American system. Though many of my points were valid, most of them saw it as an attempt to impose things on them by trying to make Creative Tech an American company," Marshal said further.

"In hindsight, I think I should have spent a lot more time with the existing employees to take them on-board for my plans. My fear was that if I spent too much time with them, I would become one among them. Then I couldn't transform the organization," Marshal said.

"You know the famous Peter Drucker quote 'the culture eats the strategy for breakfast'? I saw that in action right in front of my eyes".

"Another point of contention was the leadership team hiring," Marshal reflected on the earlier days.

"It is considered natural to hire your trusted lieutenants from previous organizations; was it not the best approach in this case?" Monica asked.

"I hired them, thinking I had a trusted relationship with them to get things executed without being asked too many unnecessary questions. However, with time I realized that this team further alienated me from the ground level development in the company. They knew me so well, they always filtered things as per my likes and dislikes. Though this made my work frictionless, it was always an incorrect picture that I was getting," Marshal replied.

"When the game changes, the players should change as well. The executives who worked with me earlier performed well in a different context with different set of rules. Creative Tech was as new to them as it was to me. And the sad part was, majority of them left me even before I left Creative Tech as CEO. I was surprised by their untimely departure."

"Possibly, they saw the dichotomy more clearly. They saw that there was a big disconnect between your plans and the execution team on the ground. They knew it was a lost battle," Monica concluded.

"Did excessive media interest help in your plans or jeopardize it?" Monica asked Marshal.

"To be frank, I enjoyed the media attention in the beginning. They lapped up every word that I said. It was nice to see newspapers discussing our future plans and how we planned to reinvent ourselves.

"But slowly they started becoming noisy and published some of the gossips through secretive leaks. One column would be contradicted by another eminent column and suddenly everyone started having an opinion on every aspect of Creative Tech.

"My learning has been that if a company starts getting reported in the mainstream media for non-business reasons, it will eventually end up with bad publicity. The media coverage about a company like ours should be business like with numbers and figures," Marshal said.

"If I had to go back in time and correct things, I would probably rework my media engagement to keep them at the safe distance. They are a doubled-edged sword," Marshal concluded.

"Marshal, the employees can blame you for many things, but I must say your talk on new technology developments was the need of the day. The employees should have embraced your futurist ideas and how the IT companies would have to reinvent themselves to be relevant. Your examples of self-driving cars, and robots of the future were most apt," Monica said.

"I talk to many technology leaders and analysts. They all tell me how the future is going to change for all of us. I believed in them and shared some of the trends with our employees. To be frank though, I realized there was little reception of those ideas," Marshal said.

"That disconnect happened because the employees possibly did not know what it meant for them. They would have found it repetitive beyond a point. For connecting a vision with an audience, they needed at least some specific examples. In fact, some of the startups I work with here have very clear business application of the ideas," Monica said.

"I realized that there was not much urgency to understand the changing landscape in IT. Many of our employees refused to see the writings on the wall. My goal was to show them the right direction, but most of them were reluctant to adopt new ways," Marshal said

"Maybe to exploit the new technologies, the large companies need to operate like startups," Monica added further.

"This meant reducing centralized planning and control and giving more autonomy to smaller teams on the ground," Marshal said.

"My conclusion based on extensive work that I have done with many of the startups is that probably large IT organizations should create few independent teams of not more than fifty people each. These teams should be able to experiment on their own, generate new ideas and monitor for business performance including revenues and profitability," Monica said.

One last question, "Could Creative Tech have avoided the impact on jobs if you did things differently?" Monica asked Marshal.

"I think we are forgetting the larger context of technological advancements when we focus too much on Creative Tech. I bet you take any other organization today, their story would not be any different from ours," replied Marshal.

"Is it because of the advancement in AI? Will AI really do away with many jobs?"

"In September 2013, two Oxford researchers Carl Benedikt Frey and Michael A. Osborne published a paper titled "Future of employment" where they analyzed the probability of automation for 702 professions in the US by 2033. The conclusion of the study was startling – about 47% of the US jobs are at the risk of total automation. There is 99% probability that telemarketers, data entry operators and insurance underwriters will cease to exist in the next 20 years. The same will happen to bank tellers and legal secretaries with 98% probabilities, credit authorizer with 97%, cook in the restaurants with 96%. The list goes on, paralegal and legal assistant – 94%, retail salesperson – 93%, Tour guide – 91%, Taxi drivers and chauffeurs – 89%, construction labourers – 88%, so on and so forth," replied Marshal.

"These findings are quite alarming, are there any of the current jobs safe in that case?"

"Humans have primarily done two kind of jobs – physical and cognitive in the field of agriculture, industry or services. With rise of machines, they shifted from manual work to more creative work. Now with the rise of artificial intelligence, their creative work is under threat as well. AI will be very much like electricity. As we electrified everything earlier, AI will cognitize all the objects around, including humans. Most of the work we do today will be done by AI in the most economical and efficient way," replied Marshal.

"If advancement in technology is so scary, why don't the governments ban this! It will be for the overall good for all of us," asked Monica.

"Technological advancements do not ask for anyone's permission. If at all anything, they seek forgiveness. They try to solve some problems while creating another set of unintended problems. Thanks to technology, one day we may all have almost free energy and unlimited food. The oil will give way to natural energy sources like solar power which is practically everywhere. The solar panels from thinner slivers of silicon have become very effective. The rate at which it is growing, it is less than fourteen years away from meeting 100% of today's energy needs. This clean sustainable energy can be used for getting clean water and can enrich agriculture to produce almost unlimited food. Advancement in genetics may allow us all to live several years longer. Some scientist predict that humans may become a-mortal by 2050 when they will not die due to old age or known diseases," Marshal explained further.

"So we will be wealthy and live longer, but we still need jobs, don't we? Voltaire wrote in 1759 that 'work keeps at bay three great evils: boredom, vice and need'. It gives meaning to our lives. A world without jobs can be scary even though we get all the wealth," Monica said.

"New jobs need to be invented with new skills and learning. If we don't find the problems of tomorrow, both the organization and individual can become irrelevant. The assumption that humans will always be more intelligent than machines could be just wishful thinking. The silicon intelligence may be a serious threat to human intelligence."

Marshal explained, "Let me quote Max Tegmark, an MIT professor working in the area of AI in his book *Life 3.0*. He makes a reference to a 2007 book *Farewell to Alms* by economist Gregory Clark. The author points out that we can learn a thing or two about our future job prospects by comparing notes with our equine friends. Imagine two horses looking at early automobiles in the year 1900 and pondering about their future."

"I am worried about technological unemployment."

"Neigh, neigh, don't be a Luddite: our ancestors said the same thing when steam engines took our industry jobs and trains took our jobs pulling stage coaches. But we have more jobs than ever today, and we have better ones too: I'd much rather pull a light carriage through the town than spend all day walking in circles to power a stupid mine-shaft pump."

"But what if this internal combustion engine really takes off?"

"I'm sure there'll be new jobs for horses that we haven't yet imagined. That's what's happened before, like with invention of the wheel and the plow."

"Alas, those not-yet-imagined new jobs for horses never arrived. No-longer-needed horses were slaughtered and not replaced, causing the US equine population to collapse from about 26 million in 1915 to about 3 million in 1960."

Whether most of the employees will become like horses of the 1920s was yet to be seen, but one thing was sure, that the idea of employment was set to change with disruptive technological changes. The only way people can tide over this change is by embracing learnability each day of the work life, possibly every moment.

Just as the 3rd Industrial Revolution changed their work-life forever, this was probably the beginning of the fourth Industrial Revolution.

Epilogue
(One year later)

Rajendran had left Creative Tech after a very bitter fight with Marshal. Satvik thought Rajendran would still be unhappy and sad over the circumstances of his departure.

When Satvik met him one evening, Rajendran looked calm and happy. In Creative Tech, he had always appeared in a hurry and deeply worried.

"This is the thing about corporate life, you know – till the day you are in the middle of it, you think it's the only world you live in, nothing exists beyond that. From morning to evening you only think about work. Sometimes you think you can't exist without it and it can't exist without you. However, the day you leave your company, you wonder if it ever existed," Rajendran said.

"Yes, we all know in the corporate world, it is very cut and dry. No one is indispensable, the show goes on."

This used to be a clichéd quote on leadership transition.

"I had spent a long time in Creative Tech to secure financial stability. I was not worried about my finances after working for more than two decades. In fact, I felt liberated from the trap of daily bitterness and negativity," Rajendran said.

"It helped me to think about what else I wanted to do in life. I had always wanted to get back to academics and teach in a college. The last few months I have been teaching operations management in a nearby college. I have ample time to think about more creative and useful things."

"To tell you the truth, though I left on very bitter terms, I never thought about Marshal again," Rajendran went on.

"It is really good to know that." Satvik was surprised.

"Are you in touch with Marshal? What is he up to after his Creative Tech stint?"

"Marshal has not been in the news at all. He has not taken up any leadership role after Creative Tech. The media has forgotten about him and I hope he is having a peaceful time that he very much deserves," Rajendran replied.

"Just as all of us needed to discover ourselves to find meaning in the new world, probably Marshal will be doing something similar," Satvik replied.

After Marshal left the company, Satvik had thought he should consider going back to Creative Tech. After all Marshal was the reason for his exit. However, last few months of learning and exploration had created a hunger in him. He wanted to do something different.

"Where do you start in the startup world? How do you get the right idea?" Satvik asked Vikas.

"I have discovered that finding the right problem is the most important thing. Strangely, we are all trained to solve problems and not identify problems."

"But how do you find opportunities in those problems?" Satvik asked.

Vikas replied, "Problems and opportunities are always there around us. It is our perspective and willingness to look at them that matters. Let me explain that with an example.

"Once a manager of a shoe company sent his two salesmen to a village to explore the market potential of footwear. When the first salesman returned, he said,

'It is a very poor village. People don't have enough money to buy shoes. There is absolutely no way we can sell our products here. The market potential for our product is zero.

The second salesman gave a completely different report though.

'In this village, almost no one wears footwear. This presents a huge opportunity for our products. If we can create affordable, rightly priced footwear, it can open up a huge market for our stagnating sales numbers'."

Satvik understood the message from the story. He realized that there was no dearth of opportunities around. What one needed was the passion and strong motivation to go through ups and downs of the journey. All along, Satvik had been a stability seeker. This was the time to try out different things.

Satvik thought, in an emerging market like India, there were plenty of opportunities. One of them was in the area of small mom and pop shops. While the large corporates had easy access to credit, the same was not true for these small shop owners. The large corporates had sophisticated ERP systems that automated many of their repetitive work. They had advanced inventory management systems that could optimize the working capital. The bank provided loans to them on better terms as the assets and liabilities were well documented.

The small shop owners, on the other hand, still managed their business on paper and sometimes lacked knowledge and access to right resources. The banks were reluctant to extend credit as they did not have enough verifiable information about their assets. If Satvik could build a cloud based inexpensive solution that helped them manage the internal operations of their shops end-to-end and optimize them, they could well compete with some of the e-commerce portals. The banks would extend credit as they would know the asset positions in real-time and do on-line risk assessment. The shops could also collaborate with each other and find the most optimal buying and selling prices.

Satvik visited some of these small shops to understand how they operated. This whole experience was so different from his Creative Tech days when the strategy department would look for market analysis and run some models to understand the market potential. Since Satvik did not have access to those reports anymore, he decided to meet some of these people and tried to understand the problems.

He understood that they were quite abreast with mobile application usages. They were already using that extensively in their personal lives. With very little training, they all could adopt the new age mobile solutions to manage their business as well. This could possibly help their business grow and also create a sustainable revenue model for a marketplace-like platform.

Since Satvik was working with end-users directly, it was a direct validation of his work. Small things like local adaptations happened much better in this approach. The adoption increased with word of mouth and people in several small towns started using the solution in no time.

Neeraja was not at all convinced. She asked, "Is this a profitable venture to create digital solution for people who live in small towns? They may not have enough money to pay."

Satvik said, "We also started with the same premise but wanted to check this first. Do you know even in remote towns all these consumer goods companies have been able to successfully sell their products like soaps, biscuits, chocolates and what not? The mobile companies have been able to sell them as well. So there is definitely a market for consumer goods. So why not for digital solutions?"

Within six months, the platform adoption increased to ten cities. Though there was no profit yet, they had a substantive number of small shop owners onboard. Satvik had created a small team in the process. They started getting some media coverage.

Satvik's approach to development was very simple – their small team would meet few shop owners every day and talk about the new features they were building. Satvik would collect the feedback while some of the engineers coded for him. It was a truly agile development in practice. As their client base increased, their confidence and belief in the solutions increased many folds.

Creative Tech meanwhile had disappeared from Satvik's mind. Venkata who was the next CEO seemed more grounded and ran the company as more of a business. For the media, it was a boring company to cover now.

Satvik was surprised when he got a call from the CEO's office.

"We have heard good words about your startup, congratulations!" Venkata said.

"We have identified working with startups as a key area of the company growth. Looking at your current work, we believe it will greatly complement Creative Tech. I have spoken to my management team as well. We would like to collaborate, even to the extent of buying some stake in your company to support your venture," Venkata said further.

Satvik could not believe it. It was an offer of investment into his few months old startup from none other than his parent company. He was elated.

"How much are they offering you as an investment?" Neeraja asked Satvik.

"Well, 3.5 crores to buy a stake of 85%," replied Satvik.

"I can't believe it. Our dream has come true. We can buy our house, go on holidays and spend the rest of our lives in luxury. And you will also have a job in Creative Tech. Don't think about it much Satvik – just say yes."

"Aren't you happy that our dream has become a reality?" asked Neeraja again, sensing that Satvik was lost in thought.

Satvik replied by quoting a small story from the book, *The Alchemist* which he had read recently.

Santiago is set out to pursue his personal legend and get to Egypt. He gets robbed by thieves and has no money to continue his journey. One day he meets a crystal merchant and starts working in the crystal shop with a new business idea – selling tea. The crystal merchant had a dream to go to Mecca one day when he would have earned enough money. After few months, both Santiago and the merchant become rich.

One day Santiago wakes up early and says, "We have enough money, you can go to Mecca now and I can go back to my city and buy more sheep."

"I will not go to Mecca, and you will not go home"

"How do you know that?"

The merchant says, "Maktub" which means "it is written."

Satvik thought over the proposal for days. He discussed all the pros and cons. Satvik recalled the lesson of lifelong employment of his father, but he had moved beyond that already. Not because he wanted it that way, but because the world around him had changed. There were no more companies like Tata from his childhood town of Jamshedpur, and no father-son duo working in the new age companies.

The Creative Tech proposal was great, but the newly found experience at his new startup was even greater. Satvik had undergone a metamorphosis over the last few months. The digital disruption that sounded scary earlier seemed welcoming.

Satvik thanked Venkata for his offer and went back to his small one room office for another day of exciting, unpredictable and unstable venture. It was going to be a fun-filled journey.

Recommended Reading

THE LEGENDS OF A STARTUP GUY
Prachi Garg

Ganesha is jovial, intelligent and the youngest in the family. A foodie by heart and laid back by nature, he always looked for ways to make life easier. Despite being financially sound, with a good education and environment to back him, he has to battle through immense identity crisis under the shadow of his very accomplished brother and parents.

Under layers of perfection, benevolence and jovial extravaganza was a young boy battling to be found for who he really was.

The Legends of a Startup Guy is a tale of someone who was born with a silver spoon and yet, decided to write his own destiny, on his own terms and to bring meaning to his existence out of the shadows of his lineage. It is the story of how an entrepreneur is born, the story of his challenges, and his actions to sail through them.

Prachi Garg is an author, motivational speaker, and an entrepreneur. She is a founder of ghoomophiro.com, and has previously authored bestselling books – *Superwomen*, *SuperCouples* and *SuperSiblings*.

ISBN: 978-9387022546; Pages: 176; Binding: Paperback; Price: INR 175/-

5 QUESTIONS OF THE INQUISITIVE APES

Subhrashish Adhikari

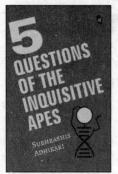

This book discusses five profound questions whose answers will lay the foundation of future stories.

- How we came to be? Was it a chance episode, or were things pre-determined?
- How we make sense of the universe around us? Are we hallucinating reality?
- Is sex bad? Are we naturally monogamous?
- Who are we? Is there a unique us?
- How to be happy? Can we hack our brain and control the bio-chemicals?

Subhrashis is a geologist holding double masters from IIT-Kharagpur and IIT-Bombay. Currently working as a team-leader in a multinational company, he has been involved in key hydrocarbon discoveries in India and abroad.

ISBN: 978-9387022546; Pages: 176; Binding: Paperback; Price: INR 175/-

LIFE IS WHAT MATTERS

Alka Dixit

When the author first met the enigmatic Dr Aditi, she was intrigued by her profound understanding of life. This is an incredibly motivating tale of a girl who embraced her imperfections and succeeded in life, against all odds. With mantras for living a better life, this book is a treasure.

Dr. Alka Dixit is a practicing doctor and faculty in a medical college in Delhi NCR. She has been guiding people to live a better life by drawing inspiration from her as well as others' life experiences.

ISBN: 978-9387022188; Pages: 168; Binding: Paperback; Price: INR 195/-

LOVE A LITTLE STRONGER

Preeti Shenoy

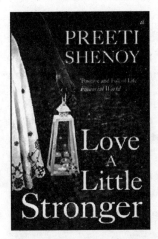

Packed with her hilarious narratives, poignant observations and a writing style loved by millions across the world, this book is certain to strike a chord with anybody who has children or who has been a child, themselves. It is a heart-warming, hilarious and inspiring collection of true anecdotes from the author's life, telling us to Love A Little Stronger, no matter what happens.

Preeti Shenoy is the bestselling author of Life is What You Make It and nine other titles. She is among the highest selling authors in India.

ISBN: 978-9387022133; Pages: 176; Binding: Paperback; Price: INR 175/-

WITH A PINCH OF SALT

Jas Anand

It is based on observation of funny tendencies in people and then creating fictional caricatures and anecdotes around them. The tendency of beating around the mulberry bush has been converted into a fictional character called 'Simon Satellite'. And yes, there are many more such characters and anecdotes, served With a Pinch of Salt.

Jas Anand is an avid traveller, voracious reader, part time writer and a full time propagator of positive thinking.

ISBN: 978-9382665137; Pages: 188; Binding: Paperback; Price: INR 120/-

65 COLOURS OF RAINBOW

Smit Kapila

There is a wonderful saying: "The happiest people in the world are not those who have no problems, but those who learn to live with things that are less than perfect."

In this highly competitive world, life of corporate work-force is full of all kinds of strain and stress. There is no way we can escape from our jobs and its work pressure, but we can certainly counter it by enriching the fun and laughter quotient at work.

65 Colours of Rainbow is a collection of sixty-five short stories and caricatures based on real life, work-related incidents. This pleasingly warm collection writes with terrifying compassion about the things that matter most. The distinctive narrative caricatures demonstrate how extraordinary the ordinary can be!!

An electronics engineer and a hobbyist with technical publications to his credit, **Smit Kapila** leads a team of world class engineers with one of the globe's topmost semiconductor MNC. An ardent believer of work life balance, when not at work, he loves being part of nature and rejoices the same through paint and music.

ISBN: 978-9387022096; Pages: 144; Binding: Paperback; Price: INR 175/-